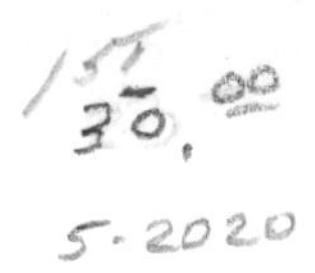

D0712898

MIKE DIME

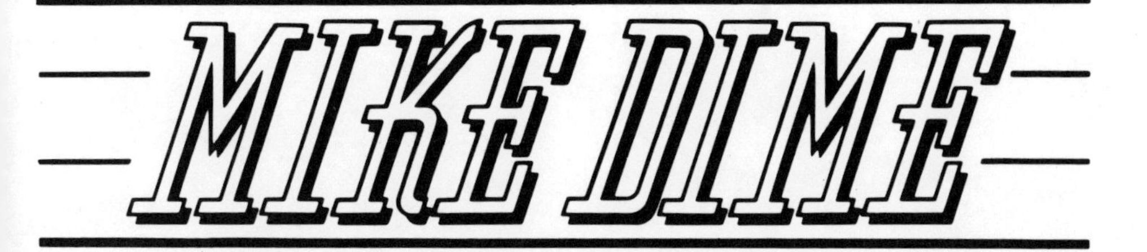

Barry Fantoni

Franklin Watts/New York/1981

Library of Congress Cataloging in Publication Data

Fantoni, Barry.
Mike Dime.

I. Title.
PR6056.A59M5 1981 823'914 80-24901
ISBN 0-531-09948-2

Copyright © 1980 by Barry Fantoni
All rights reserved
Printed in the United States of America
5 4 3 2 1

First published in the United Kingdom in
1980 by Hodder and Stoughton Limited
First United States publication 1981 by
Franklin Watts, Inc.

FOR TINA AND MAXIE

MIKE DIME

1

It was raining hard and cold out of a night sky. As hard as it knew how. Rain lashed the walls and spilled over gutters and poured like gurgling bathwater down choking drains. Rain as cold as Atlantic waves hurled itself at everything in sight, drenching it through.

I was sitting in my office with the lights out and my feet on the desk. For no special reason I was thinking about Mrs. Tolstoy. Being married to Leo couldn't have been a lot of laughs. Day after day spent puttering around the estate while the old boy scratched out another million-word epic. Supper going cold on the table. Samovars left stewing untouched.

I picked up a dead bottle of cheap bourbon and dropped it into the wastebasket. It was time I quit thinking about the Tolstoys and thought about myself. It was time to get a drink, rain or no rain.

A bolt of lightning ripped across the sky and made way for a stuttering crescendo of thunder. A pink neon sign winked on and off nonstop outside and its reflection hit the inside wall of my office. Sometimes I winked back.

A small puddle was forming by the wainscoting under the window ledge. It was getting bigger. I could have used a Dutch kid with a big finger and a lot of dedication.

I hauled myself out of my chair and shuffled through the groove in the carpet to the hat stand by the door. I put on my raincoat and hat and told the puddle in the corner I was going to drown somewhere else. Then something unusual happened. The phone rang.

I crossed the room, switched on the flat-topped desk lamp and picked up the receiver. I said hello to a woman who was having trouble getting the conversation started. She said half a word and stopped. After a while she strung a whole sentence together.

"Is this Mike Dime, the private investigator?"

I hooked a leg over the corner of the desk and hunted around in the pool of light for a cigarette. I found one under the blotter and lit it.

"Speaking."

There was another pause, but not a long one.

"It's very urgent," the voice said. "God, I need help bad."

The voice was low and loose in the throat. It spoke each word with painful deliberation, the way a child builds a house with playing cards. It was the way a habitual drunk speaks.

I blew some smoke through my nose, idly picked up a blunt pencil and doodled a picture of Adolf Hitler in the corner of my note pad. It looked like Walt Disney.

"I'm listening," I said firmly. "It's after hours, so make it brief. When people are in enough trouble to contact a P.I. they usually start by telling me they don't know where to start. I'll tell you and it will make it a lot easier for both of us. Begin with your name."

Thunder rumbled to the southwest, frightening old ladies and dogs in Chester and Wilmington.

"You can call me Norma." It was as far as she got. I switched the receiver to the other hand and waited.

Rain beat down.

"Something has happened to Frank—Frank Summers, my husband," she said between two sobs and a hiccup. "He's done something terrible."

"Really?" I said. "Tell me about it."

"Can't speak," the voice groaned. "Frank said I was to call no one. Speak to no one. Not even answer the door. But Norma got scared."

I was getting nowhere.

"Listen, lady," I said. "I am a licensed private investigator. I'm not high priced, but I'm not the cheapest either. If you are scared about something, call the cops. They'll drop by for nothing, and some of the old-timers are real nice. Like family doctors used to be. They'll tell you stories about how good the old days were, before all the changes. You wouldn't be scared with one of those guys around. I'm different. I'm tough and rude and I cost money. But if Frank is into something he can't take to the cops, I might be able to deal, as long as it's legal. We can talk about the details when we meet."

My message got through. She sobered up enough for me to wrest an address from a flood of thank yous. I said I would be along shortly, and hung up.

First I had a date with Charlie.

2

For a big man, Charlie of Charlie's Bar was doing some delicate things with a dishcloth and a tumbler, which looked no bigger than a thimble in his giant paw. He poked a wide finger into the middle of the cloth and capped the fat blunt tip with the tumbler. He twisted the glass a few times and then held it to the light, close to his face, like a man peering at the sky through an eyeglass. Satisfied, he tapped the bright, gleaming vessel on the bar and without saying a word filled it full from a bottle that he brought up from under the bar. It was something special that Charlie got hold of from time to time, the stuff that the army used to give redskins to keep them quiet. They loved it. What they didn't drink they rubbed on their skin. It was strong enough to strip off war paint. I loved it, too. It cost just two cents a shot.

Charlie was a horsey-looking two hundred pounds in a spotless white T-shirt and a knee-length apron that he tied tightly around his comfortable middle. A lot of him looked tough. His ears were small, pink, fleshy lumps and his long nose changed directions three or four times before buttoning down into his permanently swollen upper lip. His face was the color of whitewashed concrete and the hairs on the backs of his hands and his bare arms were light ginger, the skin spattered almost solid with freckles. The hair on his flat scalp was more of a silvery white and cropped very short. One eye saw a lot more than the other, but neither looked for trouble. Over sixty years old, Charlie still carried his big frame as if he were about to go fifteen rounds with anyone who fancied their chances. Nobody ever did.

Along the tiled wall behind the bar hung a row of framed photographs of Charlie punching and slugging his way through a lifetime of heavyweight contests. There were also a lot of photos showing grinning contestants shaking hands or touching gloves. In the right-hand corner of each picture, in big stage-door handwriting, people wished Charlie good luck, and all the best. On the shelf under the pictures, between a neat display of soft drinks, Charlie had scattered his trophies, silver shields, cups and plates. They were mounted on polished wooden stands and shone like an exhibition of freshly minted coins. There was a pair of battered boxing gloves hanging from a hook at the end of the shelf. They were scrawled all over with signatures, mostly of small-time pros who used Charlie's when the gyms shut. They'd hang around the place for a while, talking about the chances they missed and how two-bit managers put them with the wrong man at the wrong time and how the lucky punch took them out just as they were getting on top and all of that. Then one day they wouldn't show up and in a short while people would stop asking what became of so-and-so, and then his name would be nothing. But some of the names on Charlie's gloves were immortal. You could make out Willie Pep and Tony Zale, Rocky Graziano and Ezzard Charles.

The bar was empty except for a badly dressed middle-aged man at a table in the corner. His head was slumped on his folded arms, and the table was littered with empty beer bottles. His tie was undone and his hair, what there was of it, was ruffled and wet. His eyes, sad as a doe's, were peering over the frayed cuffs of his brown jacket.

I said nothing to Charlie, picked up my drink and took it to the table by the window. The *Inquirer's* Election Special was mopping up some spilled beer on the table. Its pages were spread-eagled at a picture of a smiling Governor Dewey and a smiling Mrs. Dewey. There were smiling hangers-on in the background. They weren't Democrats. The caption read: "The next President travels by ferryboat over the broad waters of San Francisco Bay." Outside, the rain cascaded along the street like ocean spray. I lit a cigarette and listened in the uneasy silence to the high hum of a pair of painfully bright strip lights which hung like trapeze bars at each end of the long room. I took the piece of paper with Norma Summers's address, thought about it and gave the cloudburst a few more minutes. Suddenly the drunk at the back of the room shouted out a name—Milly or Molly. Something like that. I turned to see him jerk up his head, like an alerted watchdog. He bulldozed an arm across the table, scattering the bottles like ninepins and sending them crashing to the linoleum floor. Tears trickled down the man's red face. He was wearing a badge on the lapel of his jacket. It said, "Vote for Harry." He was the kind of guy who always wore a button on election nights and always picked the loser. He probably had a whole cupboard full of them.

Back at the bar Charlie had lifted his durable body off a racing paper that was draped over the counter and was picking up a broom and a cardboard box. He drifted slowly over to the sad-eyed man who was trying to remember what he was drinking to forget. Without any fuss, Charlie bent his heavy body over the drunk and patted his back, gently, sympathetically.

"Take it easy, bud," Charlie said in a hoarse whisper. It was a reassuring sound.

"It's my Molly," the man said. "She's gone." His eyes opened wide enough to catch a tennis ball, and more water poured out. His long arms hung at his sides, like all the life had gone out of him.

"No woman ain't worth it, bud," Charlie said, and swept the broken glass into the cardboard box. There were some crumpled loose dollar bills on the floor, close to the drunk's chair. Charlie picked them up, smoothed them out and tucked them into the man's breast pocket, behind a grubby, banana yellow display handkerchief.

The man started to weep some more. Then his head fell back onto his arms, and he passed out.

Charlie shuffled back to the bar, his face completely empty of expression. He leaned the broom against the wall, put the box on a crate of empty Coke bottles and flopped back onto the racing paper. It was like time had stood still.

I swallowed the drink in a swift gulp, dropped some change onto the bar, pulled up my raincoat collar and walked into the waterfall.

From Charlie's Bar to where I parked my car took two minutes. In two minutes I was soaked right through to my skin.

3

It was a brand-new apartment block on the corner of Eleventh and Chestnut. I pulled over to the curb and parked the Packard outside an upright mile of high rent. In the gutter a fast-flowing current was dragging an unwilling copy of *Life* magazine through the narrow mouth of a drain.

I strode across Chestnut Street and pounded my way into the freshly painted lobby of Sherman Towers. I pushed through revolving doors to an area that was more or less empty except for a pile of decorators' equipment ready to go and an untidy jungle of giant houseplants that had just arrived.

There was a sharp tang of turpentine in the air. The plants were leaping out from a variety of gaily painted Mexican earthenware, the kind Californians hide dope in after a weekend in Tijuana. Dense forests of waxlike, emerald leaves were growing as big as suitcases; one ugly customer, its petal-shaped leaves shot full of holes, was just about winning the race to the ceiling against a pair of fit japonicas.

If there was a doorman or a house dick or anyone else on duty I didn't see them through the leaves. I didn't call out or find the bell or make any kind of noise. There could have been a Jap sniper in all that foliage.

I crossed the lobby to the automatic elevators and pressed the button. A carriage dropped out of the sky, the doors hissed open and I stepped on a notice saying WET PAINT. I got some on my elbow, selected the floor number and zoomed upward.

Outside apartment 1067 I lit a cigarette and thumbed

the buzzer. The sound of Chinese bells tinkled sharply from behind a mahogany door. Raindrops were falling from the rim of my hat and forming a small lake on the carpet. I thumbed a few more times before I got any action. Then the voice I had spoken to earlier called out from behind the door. First of all it said to wait a minute. Then, after much longer than a minute, it said, "Who is it?"

"Would you believe me if I told you?" I said.

Mrs. Summers thought about it.

"My husband said I was to open the door to nobody," she said from the back of her throat.

"That's going to make getting in a problem," I said.

"I can't understand what you're saying," she said. Something dropped on the floor. It sounded the size of an empty gin bottle.

I undid my raincoat and took my wallet from my inside pocket. I found a card with my name and address and the words *Private Investigator* and shoved it under the door.

There was another long pause.

"If you read with glasses," I said, "go and get them."

The time she took to read the card wasn't longer than the time it took Lindbergh to cross the Atlantic. Finally the bolts were pulled back, the chains unlocked and the heavy door swung open.

Frank Summers's wife was on the wrong side of forty and the thin side of healthy. She was wearing an eau-de-nil satin housecoat and not much underneath. She had a high forehead and a lot of untidy Titian red hair that would have looked stunning once. Now it shot out in all directions in matted, uncombed strands with split and brittle ends. It may have been a shade deeper at one time. It would always have been neater. Her face was a mask of terribly white dry skin pulled tight over high cheekbones and a firm, round chin. They told the story of a once handsome woman. Her eyes were sunk into dark hollows and may have been green, but I couldn't see that far. A row of small lines rimmed her thin lips, and darker lines ran from the corners of her eyes into deltas. A day in front of a vanity mirror would hide most of the defects. But it wouldn't hide the fear.

"Come in," she said thickly. "Make yourself . . ." There was a pause. Then she remembered. ". . . at home."

I took off my hat and she fumbled around with the lock before pointing beyond the reception hall to the lounge.

"Follow Norma," she said. "I'll get you something to keep out the cold."

The living room was partly out of *House Beautiful*. Most of it was out of a cocktail shaker. It looked like it had just housed the Skid Row convention. A distillery of empty bottles and ashtrays overflowing with cigarette butts were the central features. A trail of stockings, shoes and underclothing led through an open door to what was either the bathroom or the bedroom.

Norma Summers wobbled across the living room on an unsteady pair of thin legs that tapered dramatically into carpet slippers that looked like powder puffs on heels. She stopped at a huge walnut-veneered liquor cabinet that was awash with a battlefield of swizzle sticks, soda siphons, can openers, ice buckets, olives, cherries, corkscrews, knives of all kinds, sliced lemons, and shakers. It had everything but a drink. Mrs. Summers grimaced and waved a defeated hand at the mess.

"Crazy," she said. "There was a glass of giggle water here a minute ago. Had your name on it." She hiccupped and let out a dainty sigh. "Make yourself at home," she said again.

I removed a nylon stocking from the seat of an easy chair and sat down.

The center of the room was filled by a four-seated, seal gray velvet sofa that Norma Summers had re-covered in gin stains. She planted herself with some difficulty on the arm of the sofa and tried to get me in focus. The flap of her housecoat fell open as she attempted to cross her legs. It let more thigh through than it should have, but her thighs were never going to bother me, and she was beyond bothering about anything but the next drink.

The room was lit by a solitary table lamp, only it wasn't on the table. It lay sideways on the wall-to-wall. The base was an imitation Greek urn, but the cracks were genuine. The light threw up grotesque shadows of the haphazard arrangement of furniture onto the plain café-au-lait walls. Like a tall mountain, the silhouette of Norma Summers rose above the other shapes and made an ironic contrast with the fragile and withdrawn woman staring empty-eyed at a point on my necktie.

I said nothing and pulled out a pack of cigarettes. I gave one to Norma Summers, lit it in a crouching position and sat back down in my chair. I got one going myself, and we both blew smoke into the already solid air. With her spare hand she raked a claw of bony fingers through her hair and began to speak. Maybe it was to me.

"We had it swell, Frank and me. It was going real good." She sucked in some smoke. "I got the breaks early. I was a looker. Heads spun, *Vogue, Shmogue,* you name it, mister, I had them busting the goddamn door down to get snapping." Her voice was hollow, empty, yet somehow there was no bitterness or self-pity.

"There wasn't a big name anywhere with a Leica and an unexposed reel of film who didn't get in line. And I was good. I could do anything they asked and more besides. Dreamy lips for Revlon one day, a cute pair of legs for a snazzy two-piece bathing suit the next. Every day different and every day on top of the job. I was the darling of the little glass eye, the queen of the shutter. What did I care if the cheese schmoes only used me to step up to the big time and all those phony awards the razzle-dazzle world of glamour hands out? That was their affair. I had a first-class ticket to anywhere I wanted, and all I had to do was watch the birdie."

I got the feeling she had told her story before. To a lot of people on the way down. And often to herself. She stubbed the half-finished cigarette into a pyramid of butts and threaded her way through the tables and chairs to a floor-to-ceiling window that ran almost the length of the far wall. The heavy floral drapes were not drawn and exposed a vast sheet of rain-spattered glass. Mrs. Summers looked out at the rivulets of water racing across the smooth reflective surface and saw her face mirrored in the night.

"Then it went wrong." She shivered and rubbed her angular shoulders with her arms crossed in front of her.

I sat silently in my soggy raincoat, holding my soggy hat and flexing my soggy toes.

"The war, the booze, the fast life. I didn't know which was to blame the most. I guess it was all of them, and a few more." She let out another long sigh and rocked a little.

"Anyhow," she went on. "Frankie boy and me fell off the end of the balance sheet. The good times were as good as over."

She turned around and staggered hopefully over to the liquor cabinet. She fished around and found a tumbler with some half dead whiskey in the bottom. She practically swallowed the glass sucking out the dregs. She put the tumbler on the edge of the open flap on the cabinet and wobbled back to the arm of the sofa.

"All this costs dough. Me, I cost dough. Everything costs dough. You know how it is?"

I said I knew how it was. I was also beginning to wonder what I was doing there apart from developing pneumonia.

"I was washed up, mister what-ever-your-name-is," she said aggressively, like I wasn't going to believe her.

"Dime," I said.

"The good times were good and the bad times were looking real bad," she croaked. Her voice sounded like a very old gramophone recording. Hard and scratchy. Distant and very worn. "The kind of extras I got used to cost more than panhandling matches in the street brings home. And that's what Frank and me was facing. Because, let me tell you, I was washed up good and proper."

In the next apartment Norma Summers's neighbors were holding an election party. An agile saxophone section chasing an impossible riff warbled through the walls, and the monotonous, leaden thump of dancing feet shook the floor, rattled the glasses and capsized the oil paintings.

"But Frank had other ideas," Norma Summers continued, raising her voice above the din. "When the phone stopped buzzing for Norma, Frank did his bit. Like he always said he would. He found a desk and started pushing a pen. He damn well pushed it. Overtime. You name it—weekends, on the bus, late nights. We was up and staying there. That was what Frank said. You need two things to make a desk job pay: a white shirt on Monday morning and more slog than a backwoodsman. Frank had both, and more besides." She leaned forward and looked at me with clear eyes for the first time. She said, "He was as good as his word and here we are. All thanks to Frank."

Next door the trumpet section joined the reeds on the wax, and the dizzy, frantic noise got between me and Mrs. Summers like a thick velvet drape.

She raised her voice a couple of decibels.

"Friday nights Frank has off. Comes home just a little loaded. Drinks with the pals. Takes it easy. Who can blame him?"

"No one I know," I said. She didn't hear.

"He uses the Three Sixes, a plush bar somewhere behind Rittenhouse Square that caters to the executive trade. Like I said, he comes home a teeny bit whacked sometimes, but never late. If he's going to change his plans, he calls me. Always. Doesn't like to leave Norma on her own after midnight. Frank's a good man. Straight. Regular as a Swiss clock."

I thought she was going to cry, but she pulled out of it.

"But the briefcase wasn't his."

Then she let go. The words exploded into a bout of violent weeping. I got the feeling that a lot of the tears were for Frank, and a lot more were for herself.

When she was at the sniveling stage, she started looking in the pockets of her housecoat for something to blow her nose on. It would have taken longer than finding another drink, and she settled for rubbing away the tears with an upward shove of the heels of her hands. I still didn't know what I was doing there, and from the way it was going there was no certainty I would find out. The briefcase seemed to be a promising line of investigation, so just in case Norma Summers was about to recite "The Rime of the Ancient Mariner" I took the lead.

"The briefcase," I said loudly. "It wasn't your husband's?" She had already said that, but my tongue was stiff and the exercise would do it good. She still didn't hear me.

"Frank called me this evening, around eight. Maybe earlier. Maybe later. Said I was to talk to no one. Not call anyone on the phone or answer the door. Told me to write down the address and get a cab. Get over there right away. Said our troubles were over. But I got scared. Looked for a dick in the phone book. Don't ask me why. You were the first guy who answered."

I nodded, sagely. "And the briefcase?"

"Packed with bills."

As casually as if she were telling me the time.

"Laundry or grocery?"

"Dollar bills." She almost screamed. "A hundred thousand of them!"

My eyebrows hit my hairline. I felt I ought to say something. Make a speech. Sing a song. But there wasn't anyone apart from Mrs. Summers who would hear me, and she already knew. She put a cage of skinny fingers around her once beautiful face and said, softly, "Please, mister. Go find Frank. That money, Frank wouldn't have stolen it. Not even for me."

It had all been too much of an effort. As she spoke, she slipped off the arm of the sofa and sprawled onto the carpet. It wasn't very elegant to watch, but she looked comfortable.

I got up and placed a jazzy cushion with frills and a cigarette burn under her head and arranged the housecoat so that it covered most of her thin, milk white body. Her eyes were closed and she was beginning to snore. I slapped her arm, then her cheeks, lightly but firmly. She was out cold.

There were several phone extensions. I found the one

with the address of Frank Summers's hotel scribbled on a pad beside it in the bedroom.

I found the drawer I was looking for in a desk in Frank's den. It was full of unpaid bills and yellowing bundles of tear sheets from fashion magazines. The plates showed Mrs. Summers modeling everything from fur coats to brassieres. There were some recent pictures, soft lit art shots of Mrs. Summers modeling Mrs. Summers. There was also a picture of her and Frank. He was standing with his arm around her shoulder and smiling a big, honest smile. I put the picture in my raincoat pocket and closed the drawer.

So Frank Summers picked up someone else's briefcase and it was filled with a hundred grand. So what's a hundred grand? I didn't have an answer. I hoped Frank would tell me. I hoped he was still smiling.

4

The address I'd deciphered from Norma Summers's scratch pad was Maag's Hotel, a twenty-minute drive away on the New Jersey waterfront. I was working again and feeling good. But that's always a mistake—feeling good. I get soft and a little stupid, and my weaknesses stampede like a herd of steer. My weaknesses don't make much of a list. Blondes and redheads. And anything in between.

There was a lot of party still going on behind the door at the end of the plush hallway. Cold drinks, hot dolls and a bunch of buddies. It was a swell picture they only told me about. The record player was steaming with a suicidal arrangement of "The King Porter Stomp." The chorus howled on relentlessly, reaching its frenzied climax with the hysterical squeal of high-pitched brass and thunder of drums, as the stick man pounded his traps into the floor. I was just standing there, trying to kid myself I was better off as a two-bit shamus with leaking overshoes and fewer friends than a hermit when the music suddenly stopped. Glass shattered and a girl's laughter turned into a scream. The apartment door burst open and a tall honey blonde stumbled into the hallway on a single high heel. She was wearing an off-the-shoulder, black crepe de chine cocktail number that was more off the shoulder than when she put it on. Mascara mixed with tears of confusion ran from her large, aquamarine eyes. In the brightly lit room behind her a man's voice began shouting angrily. A young man's voice loose with too much liquor.

"Let me go, you bastards," he yelled. "That little bitch is mine. D'you hear me?"

The blonde heard. Everyone in Philly heard.

"Keep away from me, you vile little creep," she spluttered, and hopped as fast as one shoe would allow. There was some more shouting and then a hundred ninety pounds of all-American college boy tumbled through the door and lurched toward the blonde. His baby-fresh face was redder on one side than the other and a scratch mark shed blood on the reddest. He was looking uncomfortable in a midnight blue, double-breasted tuxedo with peaked lapels. His turned-down collar had lost its button, and a square-ended bow hung loose like a stethoscope down the front of his dress shirt. There was a lot of grease on his head but it didn't stop his dark hair from falling over his small, bloodshot eyes.

"Damn you," he panted. "Do as I say." He spread wide his fingers and angrily shoved his hair back over his skull. Then suddenly he swung the other hand wildly, like a gorilla catching flies. The tip of the blow hit the honey blonde on her bare shoulder, propelling her into a dizzy spin. I opened my arms and she fell into them as gracefully as if we were coming to the end of a slick dance routine.

"Hi," I said, as she went limp and heavy.

"Give that little bitch to me," the Ivy Leaguer snarled, his eyes blazing. He was hot enough for smoke.

"Sorry, chum," I said politely. "This dance is marked with my moniker. Besides, you didn't say please. Didn't they teach you to say please at Penn?"

Some people had wandered into the doorway of the apartment. They were mainly young men in tuxedos. Some had cigars. It was like a big fight night at Madison Square Garden.

He curled his lips back over his gums.

"Let her go," he ordered through clenched teeth. It wasn't a pleasant voice. It never would be, even when he was sober. Then his shoulder dropped and a fist took off from his hip.

I let the blonde slump with a thud onto the carpeted hallway floor and threw up a forearm to parry the oncoming blow. It glanced off my wrist and thumped noisily into the line of elevator buttons. He gave a low groan as a light flickered on behind a square of glass in the wall and illuminated the words *Call Accepted*. I thought about a sharp right hook into his belly. It was hard muscle. Young muscle, that would take a lot of pounding. But not tonight. Not after hitting the juice. He stood staring at his fist, which was grazed at the knuckles and bleeding. He swayed a little and squinted at my knees. His fight was with Buddy Bacchus, not with me. Then he tried to throw the punch again. His arm jerked forward and dragged the rest of him along with it. But the booze pulled his legs and he fell to the floor where he lay motionless as a sunken ship. I looked him over. He was colder than an Eskimo's big toe. I bent over the blonde and helped her to her feet. She was whimpering, and the vulgar rip in the bodice of her cocktail dress was making it difficult for her lovely young body to stay the right side of lawful.

"Go get the lady's coat," I barked at the rubbernecks down the hallway.

Ladies always have coats to go and get.

In the street the rain had eased off, and we walked into a damp mist that swirled around our ankles. For the first time the blonde spoke.

"You deserve a vote of thanks, Mr . . . ?" She smiled the question at me with a pair of very wide, cherry red lips that a lot of guys were going to have a lot of fun with.

"Dime, Mike Dime."

"My name is Grace Sanderry," she said formally. "Pleased to meet you." She pulled a three-quarter-length silver fox fur tight around her body. It accentuated her slim waist and slender hips, which rolled into long, slender legs. The green of her eyes was the color of the Pacific Ocean in high summer, but twice as cool and probably ten times more dangerous. She smiled again. It was the kind of sweet smile a woman makes when she wants something.

"I don't suppose you drive an automobile in addition to your admirable pugilistic gifts?" she asked. "Only I am in a slight predicament."

While I tried to translate the long words into English, she hobbled forward and leaned on my arm.

"My other shoe is back at the party," she said. "Along with my chaperone, who also doubles as my chauffeur. At least he did until tonight." She pronounced the word *chauffeur* with a French accent. It made the job sound menial.

I said I owned an automobile and would take her home, and she said she would be no trouble. With legs and lips as sensuous as Grace Sanderry's there was never going to be a time she would be no trouble. But I didn't mention that.

As I held open the passenger door of my prewar Packard I got a whiff of what Jean Patou was bottling that year. The price of the perfume told me that Grace Sanderry had never driven in anything less than a mink-lined Lincoln.

Her beautiful green eyes widened at the sight of the two slug holes in the fender.

"Extra ventilation," I explained before she could ask. "I had them put in on account of the hot summers we've been having lately."

She laughed down four notes of the scale and announced an address in Montgomery County at the coda.

I pushed down the gas pedal and we lurched off in the direction of Ardmore.

5

Grace Sanderry didn't say much until we crossed the Schuylkill and were heading west along Lancaster Avenue. And what she said wasn't worth remembering. She just sat in a furry ball of silver fox and gazed vacantly at the rain, which was falling with renewed vigor. In between the odd word she wiped away the dried-out tears and the mascara with a lace handkerchief no bigger than a fairy's bedspread and dabbed something from an amber powder compact on the tip of her willful-looking turned-up nose. Now and again I caught her examining my dark, rain-kissed reflection in the windshield. There wasn't a lot in it for her. I had the better view. Her hair was the color of bleached cornfields and fell in soft, natural waves. As beautiful as she was, Grace Sanderry was not quite a woman. Her features still carried that odd ounce of fat under the eyes and chin. Puppy fat, they called it when I was a kid. And there were a couple of places on a young girl where puppy fat looked real nice. But Grace Sanderry had skin as clear as porcelain and her cheeks were the healthy pink of a strawberry milkshake. She was at that point of transition from being the hit of the high school hop to a full-fledged woman. There were going to be initiation ceremonies for her, and I had a hunch she had already made a start on those. At Lancaster and Highway 30 she curled a lock of golden, silky hair around her index finger and asked me something I felt like answering.

"Do you know, I have been sitting here wondering what line of business you are in?"

Her voice had a light, confident lilt. It was a confidence

born of wealth and youth and being beautiful. In that order. "First I thought you might be a policeman, the way you acted so brutish to poor Rick. Then I had you as a prizefighter, but you talk much too coherently for such a person. Then, well . . . then I gave up. What do you do, Mr. Mike Dime?"

She was playing. Putting me on.

"I rescue blondes," I said. "I got a license from Saint George. Incidentally, do your boyfriends always beat you up, or only at election parties?"

She laughed and it sounded genuine.

"Rick is not my boyfriend. He is my father's partner's son. I hardly even know him." She screwed up her cute nose and shook her head. "He is awfully spoiled."

"That would figure," I said. She said nothing to that. The incident with Rick was over.

We were beginning to lose the city, cruising steadily in the wet blackness. Lights from all-night gas stations and roadside eating houses shone like beacons. I took a Camel and plugged it into the corner of my mouth. There was a lighter in the glove compartment. I stretched out a hand but Grace Sanderry beat me to it.

"Allow me," she said playfully. She opened the glove compartment and found my Zippo lighter. She lit me, closed the cap with a snap and then noticed the inscription. She read it aloud in a singsong voice: "To Sergeant Michael Dime, from his buddies in Ike's First Army. Normandy 1944."

I let out some smoke.

"What a wonderful gift," she said, her voice full of fake sentiment. "Packed with touching memories, I suppose?"

"It lights cigarettes," I snapped. "That's all."

Grace Sanderry pouted.

"Oh, dear, I've made you cross," she said. "Forgive me." There was not the faintest hint of sincerity. "I am such an ingenue at times."

I told her there was nothing to forgive and to put the lighter back.

"What else do big rough men keep in their glove compartments?" she asked mockingly. "I bet you have a little black book filled with the telephone numbers of thousands of adoring women. Let me look."

She reached into the compartment and searched around. I let her. I didn't have a way of saying no that she'd understand. No one would.

"What's under this rag?" she asked. "It smells very odd."

She pulled out a cloth-covered package.

"It's heavy," she said, weighing the object with both hands.

"It's a pizza Napoli," I said. "I get hungry working nights."

Like it was a birthday present, Grace Sanderry slowly pulled back the layers of oily rag. Her eyes were shining with curiosity.

"It's a *gun*," she exclaimed as the dull blue metal at last revealed itself.

"It's a Luger," I said. "It came from the same place as the lighter. The difference is the guy who gave me the shooter didn't have time to have it engraved."

"Do you *shoot* people with it?"

"Sometimes," I said. "I also have a .38 Detective Special. Sometimes I use that. If I run out of bullets I've got a bow and arrow and when I run out of arrows I tell Milton Berle's jokes."

A signpost said Ardmore; she told me the rest. We pulled off the highway, drove down some tree-lined avenues to where the houses were built farther apart from each other, and drew up to the curb of a curved driveway leading to a large, uninviting house sleeping in the cold night air. She put the gun back in the glove compartment and let her lips part wide enough to run the tip of her pink tongue across them. They glistened.

"Thanks for the lift," she said. Our eyes met. Quite suddenly she leaned forward, threw her arms around my neck, and stuck her sweet, hot tongue against the back of my throat, letting it roam around the inside of my mouth like a honeybee in search of pollen.

"Easy," I croaked. "I'm a little old for a necking party."

She didn't hear. I thought of shouting for help. But who would have believed I needed help? Anyway, it wasn't too terrible. But I did have a job to do.

"Listen, Passionflower," I said. "I'm a private dick and right now I am supposed to be tracing a party called Frank Summers who has bought himself more trouble in one night than most of the people you rub noses with buy in a lifetime. Maybe I can help him, maybe I'm already too late. Don't misunderstand me. I like the tricks you picked up from your high school roommates. I also like eating and sleeping and having a shave once in a while. Food, beds and razor blades, they all cost money, and my kind of business doesn't make much of that. Some do, but I'm not one."

She listened, her warm young body still pressed against me. I felt her heart pounding against my rib cage. Her breathing was deep and heavy and smelled of excitement.

"There is no one home," she said, lifting herself out of the clinch. "My parents are watching TV at the house of an acquaintance of my father's in Atlantic City. Even the servants have the night off."

I looked at my watch. It was midnight. I was weakening. Rain tapped the canvas roof, and Grace Sanderry had me on a skewer.

"Give me a couple of hours," I said with a voice I didn't recognize. "I'll call you. Give me your number. I'll call you, I promise."

She extended a maroon-painted fingertip and scribbled a phone number in the condensation on the windshield.

"Promise?" she said.

"Sure."

Grace Sanderry giggled, took off her remaining shoe and made a swift, elegant exit.

I watched her walk barefoot to a porch lit by an electric coach lamp. She fumbled in her bag for the key and then disappeared through the door without looking back.

She didn't give a damn. And that was okay with me.

I swung the Packard around and went in search of Frank Summers.

6

I was crossing the Benjamin Franklin bridge, heading east toward Camden, when the bell of Independence Hall chimed twice. There were still a lot of people on the streets. Not by New York or Las Vegas standards, but a lot by a conservative town like Philly's. They were milling around in groups, wearing red, white and blue election hats made out of paper, and overcoats spotted with election buttons. Some waved flags, some threw streamers, some set off firecrackers. They were all pretty well oiled. Now and again cars would honk their horns and people who knew each other would wave and shout friendly abuse. There was excitement in the air, but a lot of it had turned a little stale. A great big nationwide party was beginning to wind down for another four years.

There were fewer people in Camden. Waterfronts never have much to celebrate. They end up being the dumping grounds for the worn out, the socially undesirable, the poor and all the other human dross that wealthy cities throw up. It's the same old tale. Hard-faced women who scratch together homes out of damp and decaying tenements with less than the mayor spends on fuel for his cigarette lighter. Bitter men without work hanging out in low bars and pinning their futures on a lucky break. But a lucky break doesn't add up to much on the waterfront. It just means backing a racehorse with more then three legs and placing the bet with a bookie who can count to ten. Over on the waterfront, lucky breaks are what people use instead of hope.

I turned west along Third Friend's Avenue and found

Maag's Hotel a few blocks from the Camden Marine Terminal. It was squashed between a derelict movie house and a bargain store with iron shutters at the windows. Hanging over the hotel entrance was a sign cut into the shape of an arrow. It said, ROOMS ONE DOLLAR. CASH IN ADVANCE and pointed down a long, gloomy-looking corridor.

I deliberately overshot the hotel by half a block and parked between a lonely fireplug and a pile of garbage. I climbed wearily out of the Packard, yawned and locked the car door. As I did so, a thick, slimy fog crawled off the river and jumped on my back. It was solid as a slap and carried the fumes of the oil discharged from the naval base in South Philly. I stepped over something unpleasant and accidentally kicked a garbage can. A one-eyed tomcat leaped out and landed foursquare on the sidewalk in one swift well-rehearsed movement. What was left of his mangy coat was a bit marmalade, a bit black, a bit tabby and some colors that don't have names. He stuck his stringy tail in the air, pulled back his torn ears and showed me his teeth and claws. He hissed like a gas leak and stared aggressively through one yellow eye. He didn't like what he saw. He arched his back, bristled his fur, and spat. If I had been an inch shorter he would have eaten me.

I walked back to the hotel and found the entrance blocked by a Negro sailor in a thick navy polo-neck. He was no taller than the Empire State and no wider than the Grand Canyon. He was leaning against the door frame on a bent arm and towering over a small, fat hooker in a rust-colored wig. Her skin was hard and her cheeks were stained with two violent blotches of stage rouge. Both her fishnet stockings had holes big enough to let a shark through. She was old enough to be someone's great-aunt and she reeked of cheap liquor. The shine next to her was languidly opening and closing his lips around words that seemed to come from deep inside. The noise was like the mating call of a very old whale.

I edged by the lovebirds and tramped down the dimly lit passageway to the reception desk. A steep flight of narrow stairs faced the desk, and the passageway ran through to a service door, which was bolted. At the foot of the stairs a pay phone hung in the center of a web of phone numbers scrawled on the wall. Some were in pencil, others ink. Some were just scratched. All were indecipherable. A heavily thumbed phone directory was suspended by a single thread thumbtacked to the base of the telephone. Its tattered pages were open in two even halves and it looked like a dead bat.

I lit another Camel and palmed the desk bell. It didn't ring. At least I didn't hear it above the deafening sound of gunfire, tom-toms pounding and redskins whooping, coming from a room behind the desk. Through a half-open door I could see the blue light from a TV screen flicker spasmodically in the otherwise totally dark room. I smashed down the nipple of the bell with enough force to sink an oil derrick and coughed politely.

Something moved in the eerie glow. It moved slowly. It spoke.

"No use you ringing that bell. It ain't never worked and my guess is it never will."

The words came from someone sitting in the remains of a high-backed easy chair pulled up to within an inch of the television set. A face turned toward me, the light of the screen washing over a spade-shaped chin yielding a week's growth of stubble the color of ash and as sharp as porcupine quills. Watery gray eyes squinted over a pair of half spectacles. His skull was domed by a grubby woolen seaman's hat and his skin had enough wrinkles to cover a pound of walnuts.

"What's your business, mister?" he said, turning his eyes back to the screen. "You dress too good to want to sleep here."

If he'd had dentures, his voice might have frightened me. His myopic gaze was fixed on a trio of Hollywood extras with feathers in their hair who were riding around a covered wagon lying on its side. The old man rolled the sleeve of a collarless shirt up past his elbow to expose a tattered tube of cotton undershirt. He repeated the exercise on the other arm.

"I'm an optician's rep," I said. "I sell white sticks."

He didn't hear me. A cowboy was gripping a chest that had an arrow sticking in it. The soundtrack was giving me a headache.

The register lay open on the desk next to the bell. It was less than helpful. The last entry was three months old. I pushed open the desk gate and swaggered up to the old man in the chair. There was a thick brown cord hanging out of the back of the TV set. It went to a socket in the wall. I jerked it hard. Something snapped. The room went shockingly dark and very silent. I reached out to the light switch by the door and flicked it on. It spotlighted the old party struggling to pull a .45 Colt Peacemaker from the side of his worn leather chair.

I moved toward him easily. There was no need to rush.

"This gun was made in 1873," I said, yanking the weapon from its owner and emptying the chamber into my hand. "You would have been faster then. A lot faster."

He didn't move. Not even to bat an eyelid. I put the shells into my pocket and threw the heavy old gun on the floor. Then I took the picture of Frank Summers out of my wallet and held it under his nose.

"I am looking for this man," I said firmly. "And I know for certain he has been here. Tell me two things. Which room will I find him in and will I find him alone?"

He gulped and blinked but he didn't speak. He was onto something. Information. Big onions to sell. He knew it and I knew it. An old game. Almost as old as streetwalking and politics.

I found a crumpled dollar bill and placed it next to the picture. "Listen, pop," I snarled. "You might not believe me, but I can get real tough when I'm crossed. Mean as a mongoose. If you don't come clean I won't give you this buck. And that's not just talk."

There is no faster way to loosen a man's tongue. It beats nail-pulling and hot coals.

A gnarled hand flashed out and snatched the bill, which vanished into a pocket in his greasy vest. "Room 205," he said brightly. "Checked in earlier. Second floor, straight down the corridor on your left. No one with him far as I know."

He got up from his chair for the first time and felt around on the floor for the plug. He found it, picked up the lead from the TV and began putting the two back together. It looked like a job that would keep him busy.

I climbed two flights of creaking, carpetless stairs and passed a man who was no more than a shadow hurrying by. I didn't give it a thought. Flophouses like Maag's are full of shadows. Sometimes that's all they are. A powerful smell of cooking came from the end of the passageway on Frank Summers's floor. It was something Latin, bay leaves, tomato sauce, that sort of thing. It didn't make me feel hungry. There was someone, a woman, singing in a tuneless way. It was Latin, like the cooking.

I crept up to Room 205, waited and listened. The hallway was dark and silent but for the chirping. I felt for the stock of my gun and released the safety catch with a flick of my thumb. I tapped the door with a bent finger.

"Frank," I called, just loud enough for him and no one else to hear. "Take it easy, bud. I am a private shamus. The name is Mike Dime. Won't mean a thing, because your old lady sent me along instead of her."

Suddenly the door at the end of the passage was thrown open with a flourish, and a well-built Italian, naked to his torso, stood in the center. His dark eyes peered down a frosty bottle of beer, which he was tipping steadily down his throat.

I straightened, tense and uncertain, and let the hand on my gun slip out and into my pocket. I removed a bunch of keys and pretended to find one to fit the door.

Then the woman stopped singing and shouted a name. She shouted for it to close the door. The Italian turned sharply and shouted another name back. It wasn't the sort ladies get baptized with. Then something inside the room hit the wall, something heavy that bounced when it landed on the floor. The man finished his beer and, with his legs astride, hurled the bottle with great force into the room. Things smashed and the woman began screaming. Then the man slammed the door shut and a lot more things got broken. After a while it went quiet once more and I made another stab at arousing Frank Summers. I tried knocking a little harder and found there was no need to knock at all. The door swung open on rusty hinges and let the light that was burning brightly inside fall out in a long yellow strip onto the passage floor.

The room was furnished the way you would expect for a buck a night. The light came from a solitary bulb at the tip of an S-shaped wall bracket. It had the remains of a glass shade, but not enough to talk about. There was a film of dust and grease over most things. The faded floral curtains were not drawn, and half a crinkled blind had been pulled carelessly at an angle across the open window. The wooden tip at the end of the cord was tapping the windowpane and a lot of night air was blowing in and making the musty room cold enough to keep your coat on. There was a badly chipped iron bed frame and a mattress, and a gray sheet and threadbare blanket. There was a washstand with a cracked marble top and a pitcher and a bowl. A picture of the Holy Family reproduced from a painting by a Renaissance nobody hung on the wall above the bed. There was no glass in the ornate frame. A new hat sat on the bedpost and a brown serge double-breasted jacket hung from a nail on the back of the door. There was the kind of mess flies leave on the ceiling and the kind of mess human beings leave on the floor. And there wasn't much else, except Frank Summers. He was standing perfectly still against the partition wall. I took his photo out of my pocket to make sure. It was Frank okay, no doubt about it. The head was bald, the ears were large and a big nose hung over a heavy brown mustache. It was the face you see a hundred times a day. You stand next to it in elevators, at streetlights, in subway trains. You see it and forget it all in one. But you wouldn't forget Frank Summers's face, the way it was then. Not after somebody had used it as an ashtray. Not with the skin horribly disfigured by a swollen mound of tiny burns, each purple-rimmed, each blistered and black in the center. His eyes were also different. Not a bit like the photo. They were wide open with only the whites visible, like the whites of hard-boiled eggs. And he wasn't smiling anymore. Instead, Frank's mouth was open, slack, and full of congealed blood.

There was something else not in the picture. It was the handle of a butcher's knife sharpener. It was sticking out from over Frank Summers's necktie. Someone had rammed it under his chin, nailing him to the wall. There was hardly any blood, just a spatter on his white Van Heusen shirt. No more than if he had cut himself shaving. The blow had been as clean and as simple as an embroidery stitch. The blade had missed all the veins and all the arteries and snapped the spinal chord like it was a bread stick. Frank Summers had died in less than a second. I looked down at his feet. They were big, sad feet in brown brogues and didn't quite reach the floor. I touched his hand. It was quite cold.

I thought for a bit about taking him down. Then I thought it would do no good. Someone would find him eventually and the cops would come and ask everyone a lot of questions and the wop down the hall will tell them about me. The desk hop ditto. With just enough circumstantial evidence and Norma Summers being an unreliable witness, I could probably make the D.A. a very happy man.

Before I left the room I checked Frank Summers's pockets. Nothing seemed to be missing. His billfold was tight with credit cards and dollar bills. His wedding ring was still on his finger and his rolled-gold watch ticked merrily on his wrist. There was a pair of reading glasses in a soft leather case in his inside jacket pocket.

Frank's killers weren't interested in peanuts.

I didn't bother looking for the case. I had wasted enough time.

In the anteroom behind the desk a man was yelling for some other men called Jesse, Matt and Jake to take cover behind the rocks. A sudden outburst of explosions ended with a chorus of pinging lead.

"Jesse's bin hit," a voice called out.

"The party in 205," I shouted at the desk hop who was staring at the screen like a hypnotized mole. "Seen anyone leave his room?"

"Just you," he said, again without looking at me.

Silly question.

I picked up the stub of a pencil lying between the open pages of the hotel register and in the empty space where guests sign I wrote in a big, bold, clear hand, "Hopalong Cassidy, Dry Gulch." Then I pulled up my collar, belted my raincoat and strolled manfully into the daybreak.

7

An early sun was hauling itself into a high, watery sky. The pale light painted the tall buildings facing east ivory white and put a cold black shadow everywhere else. The city center was already full of people. The early shift rubbed shoulders with the late shift and they both rubbed shoulders with people who weren't working at all. Everyone looked hung over. Men in dungarees were hard at work on the city's billboards. The giant pictures of politicians trying not to look like loan sharks on payday were already being torn down to make way for Madison Avenue's latest dream. Some joker had knocked off for breakfast at a site on Vine Street and Ten, leaving the job exactly half finished. It read: VOTE FOR SPAM. COLD OR HOT SPAM HITS THE SPOT.

The streets were unusually heavy with traffic. News vans sped in all directions with headlines still uncertain as to the outcome of the night-long contest. H. L. Mencken had holed up in Philly during July for the Democratic Convention. He called Dewey "a good trial lawyer, but an incompetent rabble rouser." He had backed him just the same. The fourth estate was going to come under a lot of fire, whoever won. Besides, Truman or Dewey? Dewey or Truman? The squabbling over who got his feet on the desk in the Oval Office was happening on another planet. It was distant, outside. Like the world seems during a bad head cold.

On the sidewalks, while shopkeepers were opening their shutters, milkmen were doing their daily routine of monkey tricks with crates of clinking bottles. Along the streets garbage trucks plowed slowly and relentlessly through the piles of trash like sleepy dinosaurs in a primeval swamp. A straggling parade of unshaven men followed behind and clanged and crashed the emptied cans with more noise than a band of circus percussionists.

Small-time businessmen were already streaming into the city, making certain they kept in the race. There was still no sign of the big shots. They hadn't even brushed their teeth. That's what was so swell about being boss: you were last in and first out. You also had a golf ball in the place where you once had a brain, and your peepers were permanently glued to the rump of the doll who typed your letters. Big deal.

In packed coffee shops short-order cooks were cracking eggs and frying ham. The smells mingled with waffles and toast and fresh-ground coffee. My nostrils widened and saliva filled my mouth like a flooding river. The aroma that spilled onto the sidewalk and into my olfactory system was stronger and even more alluring than Grace Sanderry's perfume. But I kept on driving.

I turned left on Eleven and Vine, edged by Chinatown and headed south toward Sherman Towers. Something was puzzling me. Frank Summers found himself with a briefcase full of money that didn't belong to him. Nothing unusual in that; guys lose their briefcases every night of the week. On election day they usually lose a whole lot more. Paper clips, shoes, automatic pencils, wives, fortunes. One guy even loses the election. But the briefcase was Pandora's box. The answer to Frank Summers's prayer. Whoever lost the case traced Frank and thanked him with a knife through the throat. That pointed to one thing. The briefcase was illegitimate. The kind of money Frank was not supposed to know about. That made it bad for Mrs. Summers and it made it bad for me. We both knew Frank had had the briefcase. Frank also had something else, something he couldn't or wouldn't part with. There was no other reason to burn off half his face. I hadn't figured Frank as being hard-boiled. But stress can change people in unexpected ways. In four years with Uncle Sam over there I had seen a lot of scared men transformed into heroes. Maybe

Frank was such a man? Maybe he knew more than he had told his wife? Maybe she knew more than she told me? A lot of maybes. Whatever the story, my part of the job was over, and I hadn't even made first base. All that was left for me to do was to tell Norma Summers to get protection and beat it before the cops showed.

8

The overheated lobby of Sherman Towers hadn't changed much, except the japonicas had grown a couple of inches nearer the ceiling. And there was a badly overweight janitor, around his mid-fifties, who was watering the plants. A rubber pipe snaked from his pink hand and through the lobby to an outlet valve hidden discreetly behind an oatmeal-colored drape. He was wearing faded blue overalls and a tartan shirt open at the neck. A lot of chins nestled freshly shaven under a bright red face. His eyes were blue and cheery.

"Mornin'," the fat man beamed. He unbuttoned some more of his shirt, took a large white handkerchief from the hip pocket of his denims and ran it over his forehead. He examined the linen square for a moment, then stuffed it out of sight. "Can sure get hot around here," he said and sighed.

"Equatorial."

Water trickled from the hose.

"You been here long?" I asked.

"'Bout an hour. Maybe less. It takes me damn near an hour to soak these little devils. I'm just about through." His voice was high-pitched and squeaky, like an old lady's.

I stood close to the man and took a card from my wallet.

"You may be able to help me," I said, handing him the card.

He held it up to the light, like he was trying to spot a forged dollar bill, and read the contents quietly to himself, mouthing the words. He handed the card back and shifted his hose to the last tub of a short row of miniature palms. He moved with a noticeable limp, his right shoe being built up four, maybe five inches higher than the left.

"Sure," he said with confidence. "Any way I can, so long as it don't get no one into trouble. I don't do much business with detectives."

I asked him if he had seen anyone he didn't know come or go. Or strange faces or odd characters lurking or asking for the Summerses.

The big janitor thought for a while, his brow furrowed in concentration.

"Not as I can recall," he said finally. "It's a bit early for most of the folks living here. Maybe the night porter seen someone. What kind a person would you have in mind?" he asked, conspiratorially, narrowing his eyes.

"No one special." I asked him where I could find the night porter.

"Just missed him," the big man said. "Most days we have a chat before he checks out. But this mornin' he took off on his heels as soon as I showed."

"Election fever," I said, and lit a Camel.

"Hell, no," he said. "Mr. Tucker ain't interested in no election. Says all politicians are slippery-tongued vermin. No, he went home straight away on account of his sick dog. It's a Labrador; least I think it's a Labrador. He calls it Hoagy, after his brother that got killed in the war. I told him it wasn't a name I would call a dog, but I can understand his reasons. Anyway, the pooch don't give a damn."

I edged toward the elevator bank.

"Funny thing," the big man ground on. "I ain't never cared much for dogs." He turned off the tap at the nozzle of the hose and began to wind it up over his open palm and under his elbow. He limped toward the elevator alongside me, winding the hose with slow, deliberate gestures.

"I had a dog once, when I was a kid," the janitor said. "That was back in Toledo. Sure was a cute animal. He'd do all sorts of tricks, that old dingo."

I pushed a button on the wall and some lights flashed. The carriage dropped.

"I sure do miss Toledo, mister, an' that's tellin' you the plain truth."

The doors of the elevator opened automatically and I stepped in.

"You must tell me about it sometime," I said with a meek smile.

He nodded his head a few times into his chins. "Sure," he said without humor. "I look forward to it."

A few seconds later I was standing outside Norma Summers's apartment. The corridor was empty and still. Around me people slumbered. The silence they created was thick and heavy, silent as a snowfall. It was a silence I didn't much want to disturb. I took the cigarette out of my mouth, threw it into a nearby sand bucket and prodded the buzzer. After a very long time Norma Summers spoke. "The door is open," she called out with a dead voice.

I walked through the short lobby into a living room that looked like a salvage operation after a flood. Almost all the furniture was piled on the floor. Every drawer had been emptied and every cushion ripped open. Stuffing from the sofa and chairs littered the room like cotton blossoms. An elegant secretary stood without its glass doors. They had been ripped off and lay in pieces under a heap of mangled encyclopedias. A lot of the carpet was in shreds.

The next voice to talk in Norma Summers's apartment didn't belong to Norma Summers. It came from a very short, very slim youth in his early twenties. His fragile frame was draped in an electric blue suit two sizes too big at the shoulders. His mustard shirt was a shade darker than his skin and was graced by a maroon and canary tie fastened with a triangular knot the size of a pineapple. His head was covered with a wide-brimmed, light gray hat trimmed with a broad dark ribbon. The snazzy orange handkerchief in his breast pocket didn't quite go with his oxblood red shoes. The crepe soles on them were the tallest thing about him. He said, "*Entrez, mon ami*. We are expecting you." He beckoned to me with both hands, like a runway traffic controller bringing a plane toward him.

It was then I made a mistake. I thrust my hand under my arm and made a grab for my gun. Before I touched the handle someone from behind smashed the Rock of Gibraltar on the back of my skull. I sagged to my knees and fell face down onto the carpet. A sickening heat pounded in my temples as I felt big and powerful hands frisk me and pull my gun clumsily from its holster.

"Just the pistol, Frenchy," a voice like a foghorn boomed.

"Get him upright," the punk called Frenchy ordered. "And don't kill him doing it."

Big strong hands sank into my raincoat, picked me up and threw me as if I were no heavier than a rag doll into the remains of the easy chair that I had sat in the night before. I tried to focus my eyes but there was nothing doing. Blood raced through my brain. It raced in sudden, violent bursts, swelling the veins and choking them tight.

I coughed a little and it hurt. So I stopped coughing and tried to get my eyes mobile. At first there was just a blur.

"You are looking at the Hog," Frenchy said with a tight, snappy delivery. "Take a good look, *mon ami*, and do not forget what I am telling you. He is the mad bastard. Completely mad. If I give him the okay, he will pull off your arms and legs. Simple. He will not hesitate. No questions. He will do it. I am not making this little story for the joke. It is the warning for you not to mess around. *Comprendez?*"

The blur called Hog gradually began to sharpen at the edges and became a clear, definable shape. He wasn't wearing a jacket. They didn't make them big enough to fit him. If they did he wouldn't need it. The hair on his body was thick enough to keep him warm. Over the hair he had squeezed a black cotton dude cowboy shirt trimmed with ten yards of fancy white braid on the collar and twenty yards of white fringe down the sleeves and across the chest. It yelled out for pearl-handled six-guns and a sheriff's star. Somehow it looked wrong on him, like seeing a nun smoking a pipe. His arms hung lazily by his stumpy legs, his half-clenched fists dangling a few inches from the carpet. Hog's enlarged brow ridge was matted with coarse black hair and sheltered two small, hateful holes in the place where most Homo sapiens have eyes. His nose had no bone and sat flat against his broad, high cheeks, which were heavily scarred. I imagined he had a lot of trouble shaving; a lawn mower would have found it tough going. His cavernous mouth was decorated by a lot of gold and a handful of yellow stumps that looked like the shot ends of clay pipes in a shooting arcade. His skin was the texture of granite, giving his head the overall appearance of a bust Michelangelo had lost his temper with. He was holding a .45 Webley revolver. It was a big gun, nearly twelve inches long, and a slug fired close up would have left a hole the size of a pancake. But the gun looked lost in the brute's hands. No bigger or deadlier than a bent toothbrush. And Hog didn't need it. He only had to sneeze to blow you out.

His other hand was shaking the contents of a small bureau drawer thoughtlessly onto the floor. For the first time I noticed Mrs. Summers. She was still in her housecoat, huddled up in the corner of the sofa and looking a hundred years old. I figured she already knew about Frank.

"*Très bon,*" Frenchy said. "Now we are understanding each other we shall have a little *parlez*."

He lowered himself neatly into the easy chair facing me and took a stick of gum from behind the silk flag in his breast pocket. He unwrapped the silver paper meticulously, popped the gum into his mouth and started to chew. Then he rolled the silver paper into a ball between his index finger and a thumb and flicked it in my face. It bounced off my cheek and rolled onto the carpet. My head was still reeling from Hog's blow but I was getting the picture. I wasn't crazy about it. I wasn't even mildly interested. But I decided not to do anything rash. Anything that would give Hog a chance to pull off my arms and legs.

"We have been to see the Old Man Summers," said Frenchy, working his jaw meditatively. "He was the nice guy but he doesn't have the good memory. To tell the truth, he don't remember a damn thing."

"It's caused by lack of vitamins," I said at last.

Frenchy stopped chewing and squinted. "*Comment?*" he said.

"Loss of memory," I grinned. "Frank Summers . . . you were saying . . . it's caused by vitamin deficiency."

He let it go and Hog missed it completely.

Norma Summers gave a low moan. It came from the last outpost of human endurance. She had had it.

Frenchy crossed his legs and ran a finger down the crease in his pants. He had small, deft hands. They looked like they hadn't known much work other than dealing cards or unwrapping gum.

"Not only have we seen Summers; also we know you have been to see him."

"So what?" I said.

Hog opened his mouth wide. "So what?" he repeated. "The shamus says so what?" He shook the room with his laughter. It sounded like the San Francisco earthquake.

Frenchy didn't find it so funny. He lifted the cuff of his shirt with a hooked finger and studied the watch on his slim wrist.

"We are short of time, *mon ami*," he said urgently. "So here is the fast menu. I am going to tell you a little tale which has important lines missing. You will fill them in."

He got up and stood in front of me, legs astride, and slipped the palms of his manicured hands into his side pockets, leaving two polished thumbnails hanging out over the edges. The punk pulled himself up to his full height and moved his head from side to side a couple of times, as if his collar were too tight. His breath was foul with garlic. It got worse when he spoke.

"First, I will bring to your mind what happened to Monsieur Summers when he did not cooperate."

He was beginning to enjoy himself. He took a silver cigarette case from his inside pocket and flipped it open.

"You see, I have the full pack." He took a single cigarette from the row of twenty and laid the case carefully on a coffee table. Then he balanced the cigarette end-up on the lid.

"Such a wonderful thing, the cigarette," he said unemotionally. "It can bring so much pleasure. And so much pain."

He left the stick of tobacco like a tiny flagpole on the shining surface of the case and sat with his arms folded on the arm of the easy chair. Hog was messing around absently with the chamber of his pistol. I didn't mind, as long as it wasn't the trigger and it wasn't pointing at me.

Frenchy was speaking again. "Last night Hog and me is engaged in a little errand for a certain very important party. Who exactly does not concern you. *En route* Hog gets the dry throat so we look around for a suitable venue. We choose the Three Sixes, a real swell joint with the plush seats and cold beer. After a while, with nature taking her course, Hog is off to water the horse, holding this very valuable briefcase which is belonging to the certain party. That is Hog's job, to keep ahold of the briefcase. But there is a time when even he has to put it down. *Comprendez?*"

I rubbed the back of my neck and asked if I could smoke. He didn't answer, so I lit up and dragged hard, forcing the smoke a long way down. I felt the nicotine ease sweetly through my veins, cooling the jangled nerve ends.

"Listen," I said. "This story's got less plot than the Ziegfeld Follies. Why don't you forget the prelude and get to the punch line so I can go home and get some sleep?"

"Do not get clever, *mon ami*." he said. "You talk of the drama. Hog is there, in the wings, just waiting for the opportunity to make the entrance for his big scene."

I looked at Hog. He was shifting his weight from one foot to the other and flexing his biceps, like a bodybuilder about to start work.

Mrs. Summers hadn't budged an inch since I arrived. I didn't like her having to listen to Frenchy's monologue but there was nothing I could do to prevent it. Without Hog, Frenchy was nobody. I could have shaken him off easier than a blind panhandler. I could have snapped him like a dry twig. I could have done a lot of things but I did nothing. I just sat and listened and ached. It was all part of the job.

"To resume," Frenchy said, walking to face a peach-tinted mirror hanging lopsided over the mantelpiece. "Hog is in the john when all is confusion. There is this gent who is, we find out later, the late M'sieur Summers. He is standing next to Hog when he is suddenly throwing up his lunch, his supper and a whole lot more. *Mon dieu*, what a *mélange*. Everyone is getting clear of this man, especially Hog."

He jutted out a small, china chin over the knot of his necktie and adjusted the material with loving care. He smiled approvingly. Still looking at his reflected image, he continued, "Life is full of the coincidences. You will not believe it, but Frankie boy has the same—exact—the identical briefcase as Hog's. And to his *chagrin*, in the confusion, Hog is picking up the wrong case."

"*Sacré bleu*," I said quietly. Another voice, the voice that tells me it's time to go to bed, to get up or to change my socks was telling me this story had an ending that I wasn't going to like much. Beads of sweat began to break out on my forehead. I felt sick.

"*Alors, mon ami*, what a *catastrophe*," said Frenchy, turning from the mirror and tugging at the cuffs of his shirt. The sharp light of a diamond twinkled in the center of a fat, square gold link. "Once we are realizing our little mishap we immediately put out an SOS to the boys who are sympathetic to our problem. The system is perfect. Do not bother your brain with the details, but it is very soon we are tracing our briefcase to the Hotel Maag's."

"That's not smart." I said. "The handful of yellow cabs who work the Three Sixes are regular. Call their HQ and ask who reported doing a trip to Camden. Even the caveman over there could figure that one out."

I looked at Hog and braced myself. But he didn't move. Frenchy hadn't told him to.

Mrs. Summers groaned again. She was waking up, drying out and registering grief all at once. Frenchy looked at her. She didn't bother him.

He went on: "When we arrive at Frank's room we find him just about to leave. He sort of bumps into us. We tell him of the mix and ask him for our briefcase. I am real polite, like the receptionist at the Waldorf-Astoria. I explain we cannot return his own case as Hog is unfortunately ripping it to the shreds following the discovery of the mix. He is the crazy bastard, make no mistake."

He paused, as if expecting someone to applaud. Hog would have, if he had understood more than words with three letters. Norma Summers's teeth were rattling but that didn't count. Frenchy didn't let it spoil his story.

"Poor Frank. He don't have our briefcase. He never heard of no briefcase, what case are we talking about? I tell him. I say we got hot information, fresh *gâteaux*. He continues to give us the blank look. So then we are assisting his memory. That is to say, Hog is assisting his memory while I am peeping under the mattress and into the drawers. But Frank is telling the truth. He does not have the briefcase. *Quelle horreur!*"

He spat out the gum with an air of disgust.

"Naturally Frank is now knowing too much for his health," he said. "Which by then is none too bright."

He paused and shrugged his shoulders.

"So here is the conundrum. Frank ain't got the case. He had it once. But he don't have it no more. We are searching this place with the fine-tooth comb and we find Mrs. Summers is also without the case. But she is telling us that you been to see Frank. That means one thing. You are in on something we do not know."

He smiled as if someone were scratching his back at a place he couldn't reach. My throat went dry and I began to feel very cold. Frenchy removed his hat and took a plastic comb from the back pocket of his pants and dragged it twice through his hair, which was thick with Vaseline and smelled of lemon and lavender. He placed his hat carefully back on his head and wiped the comb by running its teeth through his thumb and forefinger. He nodded to Hog. Hog turned his head toward me and fixed me with an intense stare, as if he were working out how my arms and legs were connected to my body. Frenchy walked behind me and tapped the rim of his comb on my shoulder.

"The stage is all yours, *mon ami,*" he purred. "Start talking and do not forget the details. Like where the briefcase is hidden."

My mind was a blank. I thought hard for a sentence that didn't sound like the truth. I couldn't think of one. I said, "The first and last time I saw Frank Summers he was dead.

There was no conspiracy. If I had the briefcase you could have it. Whatever Frank Summers did with your damn case, he didn't let me in on it. For all I know he could have donated it to the Injured Jockeys Fund of Idaho."

If Frenchy had something to say, I didn't hear it. Someone else was making noise. It was Mrs. Summers. She had pulled herself off the sofa and was running the length of the room toward the window. She was screaming at the top of her cracked voice. Her housecoat billowed like an open parachute as she clenched her fists and smashed headlong into the glass. It splintered into a thousand angular fragments and let the falling woman through. The scream died on the air as Frank Summers's widow took the short way down to the concrete sidewalk ten floors below. For a second that lasted an hour we all stood open-mouthed, gaping at the jagged edges of the hole in the window, which rose and fell unevenly like the Himalayas, their peaks capped with glistening blood.

Frenchy swallowed hard.

"Christalmighty," he said at last. "We beat it *tout rapide*. Hog, you crazy bastard. Put the joker to sleep."

Hog did as he was told.

9

Red darkness. Buzzing. The sound of angry wasps. Consciousness was beginning to float back slowly, like flotsam on a lazy tide. I could smell the faint odors of gasoline and leather. The sound I could hear was rubber spinning at speed on wet pavement.

Instinct told me to keep perfectly still and leave my eyes closed. I wondered what the rest of me was doing. My hands were still there, but they were tied behind my back. I still had feet. But they were not tied. I was moving. But not with my feet. My means of transportation was probably a sedan, although it could have been almost anything on wheels. Anything except maybe roller skates.

I kept quiet and listened. I could hear the windshield wipers working hard ahead of me and felt the presence of a body to my left side. I could smell it next to me. It smelled of stale garlic and lemon and lavender.

That meant Hog was driving.

As consciousness became more or less complete, I was aware of something sticking in my ribs. It felt solid, like the tip of Hog's Webley.

I started counting the seconds, and the seconds became minutes. We didn't slow down and we didn't turn. My guess was that we were on an express road. Probably a highway. I wanted to open my eyes but I didn't dare. I figured the hoods thought I was still cold and I let them believe it. I was no trouble as dead cargo and it gave me time to think.

After a while someone spoke. It was Hog.

"Is the cutie still K.O.?" he asked in a voice loud enough to wake a Supreme Court judge after lunch.

"Sure," Frenchy replied, flat-mouthed. "Turn on the radio," he added impatiently. "I hate it out of the town. The trees give me the creeps."

There was a click and the thin hum of the car radio blossomed into a loose-jawed Republican getting overheated about the way Ohio had voted.

"Shoot that crap," the voice next to me growled, "and find the jazz. Something coochy-coochy."

The dial moved through a lot of static and electronic warblings and finally settled on a bebop combo destroying the middle eight bars of "All the Things You Are." Jerome Kern would have gotten an ulcer trying to recognize the bits that came after. An alto sax started doing bird calls while the trumpet player was having fun in another key. The pianist was playing in mittens and the bass player had fallen asleep. There were five musicians and ten tempos. At bar a hundred-ninety-one-and-a-half, the drummer brought the mess to an abrupt end by hitting the cymbal with a sledge hammer and firing a machine gun into the snare drum.

I had no idea how long we had been on the road but the car interior was solid with the airless monotony produced by any automobile journey over an hour. The atmosphere was heavy and sullen, thick enough to scoop up and spread on bread. None of us had slept the previous night. But as the radio droned on with advertisers telling their low-keyed lies about shampoo and the jazz combo rambling rhythmically around unrecognizable melodies, the mood in the speeding car turned pleasantly relaxed. Like it is after supper for two and a bottle of wine.

It was nearly time for me to make a move. But the timing had to be perfect.

Then I got the cue. The Frenchman next to me said, "Damn and hell. I am leaving my cigarettes *chez* Summers. Give me a smoke, for chrissakes."

The big gun that had been prodding my rib cage suddenly went slack as Frenchy put it down and leaned forward to receive the cigarette. In one complete movement I opened my eyes, pushed down on my heels and threw the full weight of my 168 pounds behind my forehead, which I slammed like a clenched fist into Frenchy's astonished mouth. It was a clumsy blow—most of my scalp hit his nose—but it did the trick. Frenchy dropped the gun on the seat, blood streaming from his mouth and nose. But he was still in the fight. A lot tougher than he looked. He had squealed like a kicked pup when I made contact and almost blacked out. But now he was coming back hard. Punching blindly. Hog was powerless, stuck at high speed in the fast lane of a three-lane highway with cars on both inside lanes. There was nowhere to go but straight ahead. Frenchy and I struggled for the gun in a frenzy of sweating fingers, clawing desperately, like women at a hat sale. Somehow I won. I clasped my wet hand tight around the grip, threaded a finger through the trigger guard and pressed my body heavily on Frenchy, flattening him on the seat, which was now slippery with his blood. With my hands behind me I had no way of knowing where the weapon was aimed. It could have been at the gas tank, it could have been at my foot, and there was no time to find out. I was weakening and Hog was dying to get into the scuffle. We were in a prewar Buick Century, the first Buick to have a name in place of a number. It was a fast car and very roomy. Then I remembered. The gas tank was directly in the line of fire of the gun I was holding in my right hand.

I turned my wrist through a ninety-degree angle and started pumping the trigger away from the gas. I fired four times. The deafening blasts from the large-caliber gun rocked the carriage on its springs and filled the interior with coils of sour smoke. Frenchy screamed into my ear, which was rubbing against his bleeding mouth. Two slugs had drilled their way through his left leg. A third did nothing. The fourth was on target. It penetrated a lot of car leather, pressed through steel, black paint and polished wax, and ended up in the right rear tire, ripping it to shreds. The Buick went into a violent, uncontrollable skid. Hog furiously hammered the brake pedal with the ball of his overgrown foot and pulled frantically at the steering wheel, like a ship's captain in a gale. His efforts were useless. The two tons of machinery had developed a life and will of their own. The deformed rear end dragged the car recklessly from side to side before releasing it into a diagonal spin. We were traveling at not less than eighty miles an hour. Outside, the rain was so heavy it had turned the daylight black. Most of the traffic around us was either crawling or parked. Roadhouses would have been doing good business.

We hit no one on our exit from the highway. And no one hit us. I rolled into the gap between the back seat and the driver's seat and bent my knees close to my chest. It was safer than jumping out. When the car left the road, it plowed across a strip of gravel, through a high-banked grass ridge, under a signpost and down a scrubland slope. We shuddered to a buckled, splintering halt, a quarter of a mile from highway 309, in a cloud of smoke and steam.

If anyone had seen the show they didn't come backstage.

I heard some distant tinkling, like glass bells on a Christmas tree, and creaking, as if someone were shifting around in a very old bed.

Then there was a long, long silence.

10

The stars were a perfect set of polished silver pinheads in a black velvet cushion. On planet earth, Michael Dime, one of the universe's lesser beings, was getting his marbles rolling again.

I found myself on my back, looking at heaven through a space where the roof should have been. Somehow the Buick had become a convertible, with the top down. A light drizzle tap-danced across my brow and sent trickles of water running down my cheeks. I stuck out the tip of my tongue and washed the liquid over my lips. It tasted good. I did it some more.

I tried to move my body but I ached in every muscle, and the parts of me that didn't ache were either bleeding or paralyzed. Or both. My hands were still tied, and I felt wetter than a duck's belly. I started to worm my way backward in an attempt to crawl through the passenger door, which hung open on a single hinge. I slid painfully along the trench between the front and back seats where a lot of sharp things jumped up and bit me. I was covered with tiny pieces of broken glass that stuck to my clothing like sequins on a ball gown.

After a lot of grunting and scuffling I got myself sitting upright. It was then that I saw Hog. His massive head was lying very still on its side on the passenger seat. His eyes were wide open, staring right at me, an inch from my nose. Then I saw the rest of Hog. He was still in the driver's position, with his killer's hands rigidly gripping the steering wheel. It would have needed dynamite to blast them free.

I pulled my face away sharply and accidentally knocked the seat with my elbow. Hog's horrific, decapitated head rolled over, seemingly of its own volition. I flinched and my stomach threw a fit. It was an ugly head. It was a monstrous head. Someone should have had it stuffed and presented it to a museum of anthropology. Whatever happened, I didn't want it to fall on me.

Carefully, very carefully, I eased my way to the door and flopped out onto the cold, muddy ground.

The moon was full and there was plenty of light. Now and then a few untidy clouds strung themselves in a line and blocked out the glow. But they were quickly blown into transparent wisps by a fast, high wind.

Shaking a lot, I got to my feet. It didn't take longer than an hour or use more energy than a submarine needs to surface. While the moon played hide and seek with the clouds I leaned against the spare tire cover and tried to work out what had happened.

When the Buick hit the road sign, the iron girder that ran between the two upright supports had sheared off the roof and everything else in its path as cleanly as a can opener. Several other bits of automobile littered a trail of gashed earth that led back to the highway. I couldn't see Frenchy anywhere. The only piece of the Buick still worth a nickel was the radio. It was hanging by two twisted wires from the wooden dash. Between the crackles and bleeps, the same smooth talker who had been selling shampoo was now making a pitch for breakfast cereals with added vitamins.

Gradually the blood started to circulate and the pounding in my wrists reminded me they were still tied. The hoodlums had used my necktie to tie them, and the material had shrunk in the rain, causing it to bite into my flesh. I looked around for something sharp and didn't have to look far. There were plenty of jagged edges. I chose the right rear fender. It was torn and bent and about waist high. I backed onto the fender, hooked my wrists over the sharp metal, and carefully began slicing through my favorite necktie. It was my only necktie. With a little love and attention it could be made to look as good as the day I bought it at my local five-and-ten.

At last the bonds separated and I rubbed my wrists vigorously, trying to get some life back into my frozen hands.

Apart from the noise from the radio and the occasional rumbling of large trucks on the highway it was pretty quiet. A Trappist would have felt at home here. I checked my watch. It had stopped at a little before midnight. It felt like early morning. There was a smell of pine and quite a strong scent of animals.

I needed a cigarette badly and the pack in my pocket was sodden. I walked stiffly around the hood of the Buick to the glove compartment. Hog's headless torso sat motionless in the moonlight, the congealed blood glistening about his stumpy neck like a necklace of molten rubies.

I put one foot on the running board, leaned over the passenger door and put my hand into the glove compartment. I pulled out what was in there: one portable clothes brush with a moose-foot handle and the initials W.R. embossed in gold, one ornate letter on each side of the cloven hoof; three out-of-date route maps for Missouri, Illinois and Michigan, all their large cities circled in red ink; a street map of Philadelphia published by Atlantic Gasoline; a letter from Lippman and Lippman, a real estate office offering a selection of suburban luxury apartments on short leases; a half-eaten Hershey bar; and a magazine, printed in France, showing a lot of pictures of men and women doing to each other things that are normally done in private.

There were no cigarettes.

I put everything back except the candy, which I ate. I needed the glucose to help me survive the long walk to the road, to a lift and to my next cigarette.

Then I remembered I didn't have my gun. It was a good gun, a gun I loved as dearly as an old aunt. It was worth looking for.

To do that I needed more light than I had, so I took a chance and flipped the light switch on the dash. It followed that if the radio was functioning there could be some current still running through to the headlights. I was lucky. The bulb in one of the front beams shot a long strip of yellow into the night. The Buick had stopped almost facing the road, having turned a half circle on its axis in the sludge. The beam picked out a shape I hadn't seen before. It was a small and once brightly colored shape, now with its head at a funny angle. It looked like someone who was going to wake up with a stiff neck. But Frenchy wasn't ever going to wake up. He was perfectly still and perfectly dead. Behind his body lay a large muddy puddle, the surface rippling in the wind. In the center an abandoned oxblood shoe floated peacefully, like a miniature *Marie Celeste*.

I slitherd toward the corpse and turned it over with my toe. Frenchy's face was entirely covered in thick, black mud. So was his suit. So was his shirt. Even his tie looked muted. I bent down and took a closer look. My gun was stuck in an arm holster made to carry a smaller caliber weapon. I tugged my .38 free and tucked it away. It was nearly time to leave but I wasn't entirely through. There wasn't much of a chance that Frenchy was carrying anything I might be interested in, but I looked just the same.

His wallet was run-of-the-mill morocco and told me less than the stonemason would chisel on his headstone. There was a parking slip, a few hotel cards that were probably whorehouses, quite a lot of money in used bills and a photo with some telephone numbers penciled on the back. The photo had been taken near a swimming pool. There were large palm trees and white stucco walls trimmed with Spanish tiles. In the foreground a man in his mid-fifties and swim trunks was sitting nursing his stomach between a pair of large, hairy arms. A white towel was wrapped around his shoulders, and his dark hair was slicked down, like he had just climbed out of the water. He hadn't been ready for the snap as his face was partly obscured by the towel. But his eyes were clearly visible. They were dark, hard little eyes that would never change, whatever his mouth or the rest of him did. They were the eyes of someone who liked it when people smiled and answered yes. They were eyes that would never smile back.

A fair-haired girl in a light, two-piece bathing suit covered the wavy contours of a lounge chair with her slim body. One of her petite legs was making an upside-down V and her left hand held a highball. I guessed it was a highball. It could have been an ice cream soda. She was not smiling at the camera but at the man with the murderous eyes. If he liked anything, he would have liked that smile.

I put the photo in my own wallet, took a dollar for my ruined necktie and threw the wallet in the puddle.

"*Au revoir,*" I said. "*C'est la mort.*"

Then, very suddenly, I had nothing left. My legs started to wobble and my spine went cold. A wave of nausea hit my guts and I nearly fell. From the car radio I could hear the distant sound of an announcer yelling that Harry S. Truman had been elected the thirty-third President of the United States of America. I laughed and trudged back up the slope to the road.

There is always some poor guy worse off than yourself.

11

Two illuminated dots no bigger than the eyes of a shrew peered out of the night. I stood on the highway and watched them get bigger, and stuck up a thumb.

When the electric eyes saw me they changed lanes in my favor. And when they were close enough to take a good look, they slowed down to a walking pace. What they saw would frighten buzzards. But they kept coming.

The eyes belonged to a coal black Cadillac with an egg-crate grille. The car slowed to a smooth crawl and came to a standstill with its nose an inch away from my legs, purring like a big, contented tiger. Heat from beneath the sleek hood vaporized the damp air, filling the cold night with silent clouds of rising steam.

I took down my thumb.

A window whirred open and a woman spoke.

"Going somewhere?"

It was a firm voice and soft at the same time. Honey with a dash of lemon.

I hiked the half mile along the Cadillac's hood to the place where the voice had come from. I didn't have the energy to shout.

The interior light was already burning and threw a dull glow over the Cadillac's only occupant, a dark-eyed, sultry dream whose stunning looks took my breath clean out of my lungs. She had the largest almond-shaped eyes I had ever seen, with centers bigger than buttons and blacker than a raven's wing. Her irises were the deepest, velvety brown, with whites the milky soft texture of pure satin. Her wide mouth was a work of art, full-lipped and generous with turned-down corners suggesting just a hint of arrogance. The severe tone of crimson it was painted emphasized that, adding an appealing out-of-bounds note. A beauty spot no larger than a speck on a ladybird's back graced the dark skin above her top lip, a quarter of an inch below and a fraction to the left of her nose, which had a no-nonsense look about it. But there was a cute dimple sitting seductively in her squarish chin that somehow gave me the impression its owner might enjoy a little nonsense now and then. Her cheeks were very high and very wide and proud. I couldn't see her hair—it was tucked under a large floppy scarlet beret, which was busy trying to flop over an eye—but I guessed it would be devastating. Long, silky, black and shiny. A silk scarf the color of the beret was tucked into the neck of a lime green lightweight topcoat, belted at the waist with a broad strip of scarlet kid. Her long fingers were gloved to match the belt and beret. The only other accessory I could see was a set of single pearl earrings no bigger than acorns. It was a pricey outfit. It had to be. They didn't let you drive around in Cadillacs on your own in any old thing. Put together, she had the kind of rare, dark, voluptuous beauty that made men suddenly do silly things. It would make a bachelor buy a new hat and college boys take down their pin-ups. It would make married men leave their wives and unmarried men leave other men's wives. Once you let go you would be a cooked fish.

I stood there with my mouth gaping, like a country hick on his first trip to Times Square.

The woman in the car let her dark eyelashes dance once over her almond eyes. It was a signal that she was still waiting for an answer to her question about me going somewhere.

I tried to remember some words I once knew. Any words would have done the trick, but I couldn't think of one. But she was familiar with the problem of speechless men.

"Can I give you a lift anywhere?" she said in her cool, mellow voice. "I am heading for Philly, the suburbs to be exact. Northeast of Fairmount Park."

I nodded.

"Then get in," she said firmly. "It's getting chilly."

She leaned out of sight for a second and a door unlocked on the other side of the car. She reappeared and smiled. Her teeth were broad and regular and the dazzling white of a canvas sail in sunlight. She threw the gear stick forward and gently toed the gas. And without me uttering a single word, we zoomed into the darkness at twice the speed of light.

12

She drove with the easy confidence of someone at home in the cream of limousines. Somehow it made me feel small. To make me feel big again, I said, "This is a beautiful car. Hydramatic transmission and a cast-iron V8 engine producing 150 brake horsepower from a mere gallon and a half."

"Exactly," she said. "It replaced the prewar V12 and V16 engines. But I'm trading it in for this year's model as soon as I find a spare minute. It's got high compression overheat valves generating 160 horsepower from a pint. What's more, Harley Earl and William Mitchell have put on tail fins. It looks divine."

I looked around for a hole to crawl into but they don't have holes in Cadillacs.

"By the way," she said. "What are you doing in the middle of the night dressed like *that*?" She spoke without taking her fabulously dark eyes off the road for a second.

"Trying to get killed," I mumbled. "I voted Republican."

"How sad," she said.

Her voice had an almost imperceptible lisp. It was very attractive. I tried to think of some question that would have a lot of *s*'s in the answers. I thought of one or two, but they sounded silly.

"To tell you the truth," I said instead, "I was on my way home from work."

"In those clothes?"

"I'm a male model," I cracked. "I do the 'before' pose in those Before and After dry cleaning ads you see in magazines."

"And the After part of your act?"

"It's his night off."

Her laughter was cultivated and controlled. But nonetheless genuine.

"I love a man with a sense of the ridiculous," she said flatly, and pressed her toe a fraction harder on the gas. We seemed airborne. She was driving in flats. A classy pair of high-heeled patents were placed neatly with a matching handbag on the back seat.

"Been on the road long?" I asked.

"A little while," she said, and didn't ask me why I wanted to know. To pass the time I looked some more at her feet and when I had had enough of her feet I moved my gaze to her ankles. I would have gone higher but the hem of her coat was in the way.

From time to time she checked the rear mirror but our speed made it impossible to be sure what was happening outside. If you passed through a small town and blinked, you would have missed it completely. But I felt fine. I was warm again and the interior smelled as sweet as a Parisian spring.

"It's about time we introduced ourselves," she said after a while. "My name is Elaine Damone."

There was a space. I was to fill it with my name. All things would be that way with Elaine Damone. Everything to the point. Straightforward and very precise.

"Mike Dime," I said, making sure I pronounced the words correctly and in the right order.

She didn't say it was nice to meet me. And if she had she would have said it with an accent that I couldn't place. Her accent wasn't midwestern, not New York, not Chicago. And yet it was a little of them all.

"Now then, Mr. Dime," she said with an air of discreet determination. "What did happen to you back there?"

I told her some of it.

"Then you will need more than sympathy," she said. The manner in which she spoke reminded me of an attorney. She picked her words with the same precision. It was the precision that she painted her face with. The precision she took along to choose her outfits, her acquaintances, her everything. I guessed that attention to even the smallest detail was the keynote to Elaine Damone's whole style. Whether driving a Cadillac or boiling an egg, the way she did it would be just perfect.

"What are you offering?" I said hopefully.

She took one hand off the wheel and pressed a button on the instrument panel with a light touch of her scarlet-clad forefinger. The door of a walnut box under the dash opened. It was a box no bigger than a rabbit hutch but there wasn't a rabbit in sight. Just a few small bottles of very expensive spirits and six cut-glass tumblers. There was an ice tray and a cocktail shaker. The miniature bar was lined with frosted mirrors and bathed in a quiet, pale orange light.

"You look like a man who knows how to unscrew a bottle," she said. "Help yourself. Don't bother mixing one for me."

I was speechless again.

"What's the matter?" she said with just the hint of impatience in her voice. "Something missing?"

I nodded. It was getting to be a habit.

"No olives," I said.

"I'll tell the bartender," she said and laughed again. "He's in the trunk."

I told her not to bother him, leaned forward and grabbed a flat bottle of Martell Cordon Bleu. The sort Napoleon ditched Josephine for.

It was a fine sight. Full of promise. I bit off the stopper and didn't bother with a glass. I tipped up the full bottle and slugged back the amber liquid faster than a wino on the Bowery.

"Is brandy a favorite drink of yours, Mr. Dime?" Elaine Damone asked as I glugged like a baby at the breast.

I took the spout of the bottle from my lips and ran the back of my hand across them.

"If it was good enough for the Corsican Kid," I said, "then it's good enough for me."

There was a short silence. Then she said, "When you sip

that particular vintage, you can almost taste the Limousin oak casks that it lay maturing in."

I didn't argue. The stuff I usually drank never had a chance to mature. It was emptied straight out of the bathtub and funneled into bottles the minute the sheriff banked his bribe.

"I am beginning to think you are a bit of a fraud, Michael Dime," she said thoughtfully. "I have no earthly way of knowing whether or not you are telling me the truth about this so-called scrape, gambling with death in the middle of nowhere. I suppose it is just credible that a big strong man like you might slip on a banana skin and knock himself out. But I suspect there is much more to your story than you are prepared to say."

I didn't answer. I was getting drowsy and drunk. In that order. Elaine Damone didn't strike me as being someone who would weep at funerals or ask the mailman in, but she was curious about me. Maybe she was just bored, like a lot of women who drive around in chic automobiles in the small hours. Maybe I was expected to pay for the ride with a bedtime story. Whatever her reason for wanting me to wag my jaw, Miss Damone was out of luck. The cognac had been lying around too long in Limousin's oak casks and I had swallowed all but a finger. In ten minutes I would be too juiced even to say night-night.

Some more miles vanished behind us and a red light started flickering on the instrument panel, warning us the gas tank was almost dry. It didn't bother Elaine Damone. There would always be a gas station open where she was driving, no matter what time and what place. Sure enough the bright lights of a Mobil station appeared on the horizon.

As the Cadillac's hood swept majestically into the gas station, the attendant was through the door of his glass-fronted office faster than a Broadway critic leaving a first-night flop. We pulled up sharply at a bright red pump decorated with a flying horse. The attendant couldn't wait to be helpful. Big cars and beautiful women have that effect on men working at night. And most other men. He raised a finger to the edge of his sand-colored peaked cap and said, "Yes, ma'am?" He said it with a lot of tobacco-stained teeth showing. But it wasn't a face that smiled at everyone. His cheeks were sallow and deep lines ran down to his chin, like the grain in weathered wood. When the smile faded, his face would sink back into the sour sulk of a man who was forced to work nights for extra dough. He'd need it for all kinds of things—his home, his wife, his kids, his habits. But all it would buy him in the end would be a bald patch and a divorce. But I guess he knew that.

"Fill the tank," Elaine Damone said, not even turning her head.

"Sure thing, lady," he said, and saluted smartly. "Right away." When he saw me he showed a lot less of his teeth. He pulled uncomfortably at the corners of his dark blue, company bow tie and screwed up his eyes. I could almost hear his brain wondering what a mess like me was doing with a high-class tootsie in a hunk of tin that cost more than he earned in a decade.

I didn't give a damn. I just sat there hugging my bottle, humming quietly and tunelessly to myself. It was Mike Dime's big night with a dreamboat with everything a man could ask for. The attendant could go to hell.

After a lot of clinks and clanks at the tail end of the car, Mr. Mobilgas was back at the window and preparing to launch into his big number about checking the oil, washing the windshield, vacuuming the carpet and licking the dirt off the hub caps.

But the lady next to me was not interested.

"How much do I owe you?" she demanded flatly, taking her handbag off the back seat.

Crestfallen he reeled off some numbers. No big show this time. Just the gas and good night.

Elaine Damone counted the bills and small coins to the exact cent and placed the money coldly into his open palm. If there was a tip, no one saw it.

Within seconds we were moving. I turned and saw the attendant pushing his mouth around words I was pleased Miss Damone couldn't hear. Somehow I don't think they would have worried her though. No one worried her, least of all gas jockeys. She probably wasn't aware such men existed.

We rushed through the last hours of night in a not unfriendly silence and I slipped deeper and deeper into the Cadillac's plush, warm, seductive upholstery.

13

I woke up to find a slip of pale sunlight streaming between a gap in the drawn curtains. It cut nonchalantly across my big toe and dropped softly onto the carpet. Something was wrong. I did not, as far as I knew, sleep in pink silk sheets. Nor did I spray them and the matching pink pillowcases with Chanel eau de toilette. I got up, blinked and shook my head. Eyes spun, head spun, brain spun. Eyes on fire, cranium under heavy attack from liver. Blood racing through veins. Eyes bright red. Someone playing conga drum over left temple. I groaned and went into a limp, cold sweat, then fell back on to the pillow. I kept perfectly still and waited for everything to quiet down.

After about a quarter of a century I tried again: just a little dizzy. I hoisted myself gingerly up onto my elbows and took a close look at the decor. Everything in sight, from the braiding around the bottom of the lampshade on the night table to the porcelain door handle, was a different and subtle shade of pink. It could have looked real corny, the wild creation of a scatterbrained pansy with a sudden burst of inspiration after a long spell of dyspepsia. But the whole show was as tasteful as Art Tatum playing "Tenderly." And as sexy as a garter belt and black silk.

The ormolu dressing table at the foot of the bed was genuine Louis Somebody-or-another and its elegant rosewood legs seemed to grow, as with all fine furniture, naturally, like small trees out of the flamingo pink thick-pile carpet. There was a chair with low arms of the same period standing by the table, its back upholstered in a faded Beauvais tapestry showing two naked cherubs of the same sex embracing.

All the pieces in the room looked that old or that fancy. On the wall to the left of the large bed hung four deep frames. The plush, velvet mounts were a deep cold pink, almost burgundy, and provided a muted surrounding for a set of pasty-looking pastel flower studies in the style of Odilon Redon, only with a touch more decadence than the French Symbolists perfected.

The flowers on the bedside table were real. One dozen ice pink carnations stood proudly on their slender stems in a delicate, fluted glass vase the color of young rosé wine.

I didn't need a Baedeker to tell me where I'd spent the night. Elaine Damone was written in every nook and cranny.

The double bed was made up for one and covered with a patchwork bedspread. The patterns of tiny floral octagons were a subtle blend of coral and magenta. At the foot of the bed lay the only object that didn't fit the color scheme. It was a cream terrycloth bathrobe. I was certainly going to need something to climb into. Whoever put me to bed forgot the pajamas. I was lying as white and as naked as a peeled potato.

I felt my face burn a little as it matched up with the decor. It was ridiculous, I told myself, a grown man blushing. Lots of big boys sleep in the raw. Even unconscious private investigators.

Then I saw the note. It was propped up against a freshly opened pack of Camels. The message was typed. It read:

> I take it you slept well. There was no choice but to put you to bed. Your clothes are being cleaned, at least those not in several pieces. My maid is off till noon and I have an engagement. Your valuables are safe in the night table drawer. There is a full icebox and a pot of fresh coffee in the kitchen. Please make yourself at home and forgive me for not being on hand, so to speak, when you wake up.

There was no signature. No kisses. No yours this or that. Just a note. Oh, well.

With great care I swung my legs around and off the bed and put the flats of my feet on the deep woolen carpet. I got up slowly and stumbled into the bathrobe, which fit like it was tailor-made. I checked the label. It was English, from somewhere called Liberty's, with a London address.

My head was still very heavy and my mouth dry as tumbleweed. I sat back down on the bed, shook a cigarette from the fresh pack and located my lighter in the drawer. I flicked up a flame and pulled hard and deep.

Most people have a ritual to start their day. Maybe a plate of prunes, a prayer, or balling the wife. With me it's a coughing fit after the first lungful of cigarette smoke. It lasts about five minutes and gives my body all the nourishment it needs. Anyhow, in the alienating atmosphere of Elaine Damone's pink nighterie, it was something to call my own. So I coughed and coughed and felt like death.

Then I put out the cigarette and dragged myself over to the window for some real air. I pulled back the blush pink curtains and pushed open a rectangle of glass. The clean, top-of-the-city air punched me on the chin and gave my raw face the once-over. It felt great and I closed my eyes and just let it happen.

The apartment was a penthouse suite on a tall, fat luxury block looking east across the north end of Fairmount Park. Philly stretched out in a busy, sunny haze. Rooftops rose and fell and rolled into the horizon of purple and gray. Below, the emerald grass of the Bala Golf Club flopped lazily against the edge of the park. Pairs of men in brightly colored shirts and pants dotted the fairways as conspicuously as lights on a Christmas tree. On a peaceful strip of the Schuylkill River, rowing crews in bulky sweaters rocked their bodies steadily back and forth, as if keeping in time with a metronome set at largo. Their slim crafts glided over the water as effortlessly as a puck on ice.

It was nice not working, not that I worked that often. But it was even nicer puttering around Elaine Damone's bedroom, with all its hidden delights. I was feeling pretty pleased with myself. I had been too late to stop Hog and Frenchy killing Frank Summers, let Mrs. Summers jump to her death, and then engineered the death of two hoodlums. Not bad for a day out of the office. In a minute or two I'd look around the apartment for some golf togs and then pop downstairs and see if I couldn't bump off a few caddies before lunch.

I stopped the deep breathing and closed the window. The air was making me light-headed. It was also making me hungry. I set off for the kitchen, picking up the cigarettes and creeping close to the wall, palming it for support. I had forgotten how hard walking was.

After a few wrong turns, doors that opened into closets and large dark rooms with the drapes drawn, I arrived at Elaine Damone's kitchen. Escoffier would have thought it was okay. In fact he would have probably traded in his book of secret recipes for a chance just to boil a pan of water there. It didn't have an abattoir. It had everything else. Everything you needed from an electric olive-pitter to a custom-built Westinghouse range that could prepare, cook, serve and eat a ten-course dinner without the slightest assistance from a human being. One day they would fit it with methane rocket engines and send it to Mars.

The same guy who decorated the bedroom had been let loose in the kitchen and I would have guessed everywhere else. Here it was Old Colonial. Walls not covered by rickety old cupboards full of cured woodworm, stained with thick brown varnish and wax polished, were exposed brick. That or painted brilliant white, or faced with crude, knotty pine. A modern double sink was hidden in an ancient mahogany cabinet with its insides removed to make way for the plumbing. It was under a wide, sunny window that was bookended by a pair of starchy-looking, blue gingham curtains. The valance was plain wood and covered with hand-painted red and yellow tulips in the stencil style of the Pennsylvania Dutch. On the window ledge a pewter jug was stiff with white-throated belladonna lilies. There was a sturdy refectory table in oak that Columbus brought over and some chairs with slat backs and woven leather seats.

An old kerosene lamp with brass fittings and a crimson shade hung over the table, suspended from a thick black iron chain that was fixed to a rusty bent hook in one of the false, unplaned wooden beams that ran the length of the ceiling. And there was a lot more brass and copper hanging on the walls. Pots and pans dripping from long handles hung in neat rows, biggest to smallest and all as bright and as shiny as the chrome on the President's Lincoln Continental. Against the wall facing the range stood what the English call a dresser and what Americans call a hutch. It was bulging with prim-looking Delft dishes with blue tea trees and that sort of thing. A lot of it was carefully preserved kitchenware from the homes of early Pennsylvania settlers. The shelves were groaning with jars and jugs and all sorts of implements that no longer had a use. No one, except perhaps a museum curator, would know what to call them, but they seemed happy enough, all neatly arranged and cherished. Certainly they were never going to be used to cook with again. As I cast an eye over the room, I wondered if anyone did anything in it except clean and polish.

As a finishing touch, a kind of *coup de théâtre*, the interior decorator had thrown a splendid old spinning wheel into the corner next to the icebox. I looked around for the iron hip bath, an old stove and a scalped Quaker holding the family Bible. No dice. I made a note to mention it if I ever bumped into the decorator. Oversights like that can kill a room stone dead.

On the range a stainless steel coffee percolator bubbled merrily. It filled the room with the rich aroma of freshly roasted beans. The room was vast, like a football field. I set off and ran out of breath halfway. I pulled out a chair, sat and smoked and thought some more about the taste of coffee. Then I moved on. I aimed to get to the percolator before nightfall.

For most people the coffee percolator is a common piece of kitchen equipment that is no more dangerous than a rubber duck. To someone in my fragile condition it was a lethal weapon.

There were some cups and plates and things laid out on the table. I picked up the percolator with more care than if it were a Ming vase full of cracks and tipped the spout over a bottle green breakfast cup. I watched helplessly as a thin stream of steaming brown liquid poured over the tiled floor. I moved the percolator desperately trying to get some of the coffee in the cup. I failed completely. My hands were shaking like Toscanini silencing a fiddle section.

I put the pot back on the range and started looking for something to mop up the mess with. There were a lot of drawers to choose from. While I dithered, the puddle on the mottled white and charcoal tiles spread wider. I had got as far as opening a drawer full of table linen when the room was suddenly filled with thick black smoke and the acrid stench of scorched coffee. I had placed the empty pot back on a live burner. Lawd sakes! I gaped miserably as the percolator erupted, a lava of sodden, red-hot ground beans pouring in all directions. Dark brown specks spat at the walls and floor and ceiling and everything else. It created a mottled effect that was years ahead of its time. Elaine Damone's maid wouldn't be crazy about it, but her cute interior decorator would. By the end of next week, everyone in Manhattan would have coffee-stained walls, ceilings and floors.

I grabbed hold of the percolator and instantly gave myself a first-degree burn. Blowing my fingers and cursing like the skipper of a tramp steamer, I turned on the cold-water faucet and hurled the damn pot into the sink where it hissed and sulked like a dragon out of flames.

I was still choking on the smoke. In desperation I tried to open the window, the theory being to push up an aluminium lever and rest an extended arm on a small protruding notch. In practice I pushed too hard and put my fist clean through the pane. The shock of the sound of smashed glass and the sudden pain of two damaged hands sent me reeling back across the room, as if pursued by a swarm of angry hornets. If I'd had eyes in the back of my head I would have seen the hutch. I sailed into it like a cannonball. All that was breakable broke, and broke into very small pieces. The pool of coffee had followed me and was worming its way eagerly through the bits of busted soup boats and cheese dishes and cups and saucers. Untouched, moss would grow there in time, and tiny plants would appear. Flowers would shoot up and bees would wander by and do what bees do and Elaine would have a miniature rock garden right there in her kitchen.

It wouldn't look so bad.

I struggled to my feet and headed off in the direction of the icebox, a long way from the swamplands. In a neutral corner I smoked another cigarette with slightly less pleasure than someone about to face a firing squad, and the sweet taste of the smoke reminded me I usually drank something with tobacco.

Smoking a cigarette on its own is like wearing a jacket and no pants. The ability to locate a bottle of alcohol, even in moments of extreme stress, is a pronounced feature of the Michael Dime Detective Agency. I didn't even have to leave the kitchen. In no time at all I had found a door, which led to a walk-in pantry, which led to a wine rack, which led to a dozen bottles of very cold and very old champagne. I took one from the rack, blew some dust off and toddled back into the kitchen.

I couldn't find any glasses but there was a single egg cup remaining on the top shelf of the hutch. I picked it up and put it on the table. I wasn't fussy. Vintage champagne would taste good whatever you drank it from.

I popped the cork and poured a shot of the pale golden fizz into the makeshift goblet. Without rushing, I lifted the cup to my lips and let the bubbling wine trickle down my throat.

Taste buds exploded into life and saliva started flowing and I began to feel just a little pleased with myself. I kept pouring out the drams and knocking them back and in less time than it takes to recite Ogden Nash I had emptied the fat, gold-encrusted bottle to the last frothy drop.

With the grape flowing through my body it wasn't long

before I forgot about my cuts and burns and the bruises from the night before. I was at the stage where I could have forgotten about almost anything. But not absolutely anything.

Mike Dime was hungry. "You could use breakfast," I told myself out loud. And with a big, silly grin on my face I went in search of a pig to slaughter. I opened the huge white door of the refrigerator and found a package of ham, some fat and a row of eggs.

The last time I cooked breakfast was at summer camp. But the idea of a full belly drove me on. My mind conjured up images of plates of succulent edibles, like those that *McCall's* prints over two pages around Thanksgiving.

I put a pan on a burner and threw in some fat. Then I tried to break an egg that wouldn't break. I hit it with some force. Some of the shell fell off, but nothing else. Maybe Elaine Damone had chickens that laid solid eggs. Maybe there was gold inside. It wouldn't surprise me. I hit the egg again, with the edge of a butter knife. It cut the egg in two. The egg was hard-boiled. It figured. It was the mark of a prudent woman to have a hard-boiled egg in the icebox, just in case someone wanted a dressing for steak tartare.

The next egg I broke mostly dribbled down the outside of the pan and instantly fried into a thin yellow film, like congealed paint. The same thing happened to the other six eggs. Ham, I decided, would be a lot simpler. It would have been but I had forgotten to turn down the heat. As the slice of pink flesh touched the burning fat, the pan and the pig burst into a crackling inferno. Fierce flames leaped upward looking for things to swallow as, panic-stricken, I emptied the fireball out of the hole in the busted window and slung the pan into the sink alongside the percolator.

Then as fast as I knew how I ran back to the safety of Elaine Damone's bedroom and fell exhausted into the low-armed chair by the dressing table.

I sat there with the door closed, shaking like a scared rabbit in his warren. Chain-smoking, I stared anxiously at the door. Any second I expected the kitchen to break it down and claim its revenge.

14

I was spitting a speck of tobacco off the tip of my tongue when the pink bedroom extension phone rang. A clock on the night table told me the maid was a long way from answering it. I let it ring a while, just in case Elaine Damone was at the other end of the apartment, organizing a clean-up operation for the kitchen.

No one answered.

I picked up the receiver and waited. An oily Californian cultured voice said a name. It was the voice of a guy who hung around all day in a velour smoking jacket with a cigarette holder growing out of a perfect set of white teeth. It was the same guy you saw in grade B movies wearing a cruel smile, a pencil-line mustache and a cravat with a diamond-studded pin. The diamond and the accent would both be phony. But then so was the rest of him. All completely phony. The name he spoke was Elly.

"Elly," he said again. "Is that you?"

I started to say that I was alone in the apartment, but the moment I opened my mouth the line went dead. At the same time, a door slammed. But not noisily. I looked at the receiver and then put it back in the cradle.

The woman who walked through the bedroom door was carrying a pile of flat, rectangular boxes. Without speaking, Elaine Damone bent over, placed the goods on the bed one beside the other and then straightened up. She was damn elegant. Damn beautiful. And pretty near damn untouchable. Yet there was something different about her. It was not only her hair, which the night before had been hidden but now hung, as I knew it would, in thick, jet black silky waves to well below her shoulders. Nor the exotic, out-of-season tan.

The difference was in her smile. It was warm as she spoke. She said, "One shirt, one tie, some socks and one suit. The holes have had the attention of the cleverest invisible mender this side of fairyland."

She lifted the lid off the biggest box and held up the jacket at arm's length.

"Pretty good," I said. "Couldn't the fairies have found me something less embarrassing than my skin to sleep in? I'm not used to strange broads tucking me up naked, and I don't like not having a chance to ask them to join me."

"Very crude," she said, haughtily. "Anyway, I have servants to do that sort of thing. It took my maid an hour to get the grime off you. What is more, if it wasn't for an old family custom to extend hospitality to the needy, I would have dumped you on the sidewalk and let you sleep it off in the rain. It would probably have been no more than you deserve."

"Easy," I said. "You'll go pale with anger and lose the tan. Where did it come from, Cannes? Mexico? L.A.?"

"Wellfleet," she said as if she were telling a school kid the capital of China.

She was dressed in a soft-shouldered, stone tussah jacket, nipped tight at the waist. The skirt was pleated, calf length, midnight blue and fresh from Christian Dior's salon. It was so fresh I had to look twice to make sure I couldn't see its designer clinging to the hem with a cluster of pins in his mouth. Her dark stockings were sheer and swished when she moved. Her elegant stride as she walked to the door was purposeful and very slightly splay-footed. Like the walk of a dancer.

If it were humanly possible, you might forget a lot of what Elaine Damone looked like but you would never forget her big, black, deadly eyes. Beneath the deep, dark stillness there lurked something hot, something explosively passionate, something like an Eastern princess on her wedding night. Whatever the something, Elaine Damone's almond eyes would haunt you to your dying day.

"Put your nice clean pants on, Mr. Dime," she ordered. "If you can manage such a simple task without bringing the house down. Then join me for a drink in the living room. There is something of a very personal nature I wish to discuss with you. Business, you might say."

She closed the door once more and left me with the boxes. I found a fresh ice blue button-down shirt and a square-ended shantung tie with purple and gold horizontal bars, both wrapped in tinted tissue paper. The rest of the clothes were my own.

I ran a thumb and finger under my chin and discovered I needed a shave. So I dressed, leaving the top button of my shirt undone. I put the tie in my pocket and took my things from the drawer in the bedside table, including my gun and arm holster. Then I joined Elaine in the living room.

15

I walked through an apricot alcove into a spacious and airy room. Built-in mahogany bookshelves lined most of one wall, the books lining the shelves as neat and tidy as a parade of West Point cadets. There were a few titles in Spanish and Russian but most were modern American authors. There was nothing cheap. Nothing to help you kill time while the bath was running. And laid out like a library. You could find what you were looking for blindfolded.

A few comfortable armchairs were sitting quietly, strategically placed for polite conversation. And there were a few chairs that didn't say "Sit in me." They were modern American, like the books. Their lines had been kept simple, totally uncluttered, and were an open statement of self-consciousness. They said, "Careful, brother, sit in *me* and I'll break your back."

In the middle of a brick red carpet a giant circular glass coffee table stood on three polished legs of tubular chrome. Its surface was covered by a display of current magazines, arranged in a huge sweeping fan. It was a work of craftsmanship, almost art. In some rooms you can have a ten-fisted brawl or teach a kangaroo to tap-dance and you would never notice the difference. Not in Elaine Damone's living room. It was arranged as carefully as a stage set. If you left one of the magazines carelessly lying around it would probably climb back to its place in the fan all on its own.

Elaine Damone was sitting sideways in the window seat with her legs crossed, reading a newspaper. She didn't look up until she had finished what she was reading.

"Poor old Tom Dewey," she said, folding the paper twice and placing it in a dark-stained wooden rack. "There was hardly anything in it at the end. Just a handful of votes. He'll be so upset."

Casually as I knew how, I strolled across the room, my hands in my pockets, and gave the once-over to a large oil painting in an ebony frame.

It was a cubist affair, somber browns, grays and a lot of ugly lumps.

"George Braque," Elaine Damone said. "I believe it's a portrait of Picasso."

"It must have been the day they both had mumps," I said and turned around to face her.

Elaine Damone floated off the window seat and strode gracefully to a japanned highboy the other side of the room.

"I did not ask you here for your opinion of art. Least of all modern painting. It's a subject a few people know a little about, and most people absolutely nothing."

I let that go.

The doors of the highboy were decorated with a menagerie of Oriental herons, lions, pagodas and gardens with streams crossed by fragile-looking bamboo bridges. The doors opened to reveal a well-stocked liquor cabinet.

"What will you have?" she said politely, waving her forefinger at the rows of bottles. "There is plenty of everything except beer. I find it a vulgar drink and so do most of my friends."

I said I wasn't fussy and Elaine Damone mixed highballs, dropping ice from silver tongs into two glasses.

"Sit down," she said with a smile that wasn't exactly warm enough to melt the ice, but a shade warmer than a layer of frost.

In the corner of the room an old oak Steinway was parked unobtrusively with both its lids open. A book of Clementi sonatas stood open on the rack.

I took my drink from her hand and sat on the piano stool.

"You play those?" I asked, throwing a glance at the dots.

"Sometimes," she said. "And always badly."

I grinned. She probably gave Horowitz tips.

She settled herself back in the window seat and prepared herself for a speech. She crossed her legs once more and smoothed down her skirt by running the flat of her palm outward over her thigh. If she was wearing jewelry I didn't see it. Not even a ring.

"You are a private detective," she said at last. Her dark eyelids lowered. "This is not easy for me. I am not used to discussing my private life with complete strangers, least of all with a man in your profession."

I sipped the drink. The ice touched my teeth.

"You don't have to," I said politely.

There was a pause. Then she said, "Are you engaged on a case at the moment?"

I shook my head and Elaine Damone put down her drink. "A member of my family has become involved in an unsavory situation from which he is unable to free himself. I now believe I require the advice and assistance of someone with your qualifications. Having no experience in such matters I am relying to a certain extent on my instincts. There can be no logical reason for choosing you. But it must be said that, should you be prepared to help, I would expect you to do so within the strictest confidence. Is that clear?"

"I'll let you know when I've heard it," I said. "And I'll hear it when you stop treating me like the plumber. The hospitality here is fine but I didn't ask for it. And it certainly doesn't buy me. If you've got a case I can work on, that's fine. You can take back what I owe for the laundry out of my first day's expenses." I stood up and swallowed the highball in one gulp, ice and all.

"And another thing," I said, as her huge eyes became even bigger with amazement. "I could use another one of these liquid breakfasts and something to smoke to go with it. I'm all through with the last pack you handed out."

At first she didn't know how to take it. There was a silence powerful enough to bend steel girders. Then, without saying a word, she produced another drink and a veined, onyx cigarette box from the solid onyx mantelpiece.

"The flat cigarettes without tips are Turkish, the others are Egyptian," she said. "If you wish for your own brand you will have to wait until my maid returns."

I said cigarettes were all the same to me, took one, and lit up. Elaine Damone was standing very close to me. There was the faintest hint of jasmine in the air and then it was lost in the smoke from the rich, black tobacco. Other women had arms and legs, bits they strap to stay in and other bits they strap to stick out. Other women could dance around in a G-string and nothing else and no one, not even a POW on his first day home, would take the slightest notice. Elaine Damone would never have that problem. She could step out in a boiler suit and a deep-sea diver's helmet and waders and still start a riot. But she was speaking again.

"You would not have needed to strain your undoubtedly shrewd powers of observation to detect that I enjoy a standard of living I could clearly not afford from my salary. Not unless, that is, I were a film star or the head of a company. Obviously I am not the former. Nor, for the record, am I a tycoon. There is no secret or mystery surrounding my wealth. It is the result of a family with a long history and much financial acumen. The Damones are of Spanish origin, from Castilian stock. My forefathers went to South America and in successive generations spread north. The early Damones were fabulously wealthy, making their money first from gold and sugar, then from coffee and copper. I must repeat, ours is not like the get-rich-quick families that are featured so prominently in newspapers today. We are powerful and very proud. We are also discreet to the point of anonymity."

She shook her thick black hair with a jerk of her head and took a cigarette from another box, one made from heavy, dark wood and carved with the profiles of Negro slaves. It was a cigarette with a gold tip. The name Casa Damone ran in gold along the paper.

Her lips made the shape of a heart, opened a little, and let out a thin stream of blue smoke.

"Heirs to vast fortunes like the Damones receive more

than mere gold. They inherit an unblemished name and a massive responsibility. And the name is most important. It is, after all, the one thing that the new rich cannot buy."

She pulled the cigarette from her lips with a flourish.

As far as a lecture in socioeconomics went, Miss Damone's was fine. I liked the bit about the money. I didn't have much. I liked her getting hot about something. I didn't think it would happen often. She seemed to read my thoughts, but she didn't move. She stood before me, nobly, less than an arm's length away.

"I have a brother," she went on. "Unlike me he has no self-control. Whereas I have placed the highest premium on restraint and have invested my time and inheritance constructively, Stanton has squandered everything he has been given on a life of debauchery."

"It can happen to the best of us," I said.

She began rubbing the ball of her little finger of the hand holding the cigarette with the ball of her thumb.

"Stanton is a good boy at heart. He means well, and Father loves him more dearly than anyone else in the world. I have been most circumspect about the people with whom I associate, being aware of the vulnerability to which a rich woman is constantly prone. Not Stanton. Anyone who takes a drink from him is immediately treated as a lifelong companion. But no matter what Stanton does, Father finds ways of dismissing his failings. Wild oats, he calls them. And, to be fair, Stanton's behavior is foolish rather than criminal. However, sometime last year, Stanton did commit a crime. A serious crime which, if it came to Father's ears, would destroy his love for Stanton utterly. Moreover, Father is not a well man. His heart has been troubling him for a long time. He has already suffered two minor attacks, and doctors warn that a third might leave him permanently bedridden. It might possibly kill him."

Elaine Damone turned and strode to an early English commode that was sitting comfortably under a picture of van Gogh with his head bandaged. She pressed her cigarette into an enormous alabaster ashtray and faced me once more, her eyes alight.

"This kind of thing is not easy for me, Mr. Dime," she said.

"It never is," I said, drawing hard on the butt. "Everyone has a story they hate telling. But they usually feel better after they tell it. That's what priests are for. Tell me and I'll send you a bill. But if the storyteller has the legs of a mannequin and the hips of a Greek goddess I can usually come to some arrangement."

It was a cheap pass. We both knew it. But Elaine Damone said nothing. Instead, she raised her hand and opened the van Gogh as if it were a door. Behind it was a small wall safe. She fiddled with the dial, and with a smooth click it opened. A second later, with another smooth click, it closed. Elaine Damone had taken a fat manila envelope from the safe and placed it on top of the commode, between a sweet Lalique opalescent glass figure dancing coyly in the altogether and a silver dish with a domed oval foot decorated with sprays of berried ivy and whiplash tendrils.

"There are a hundred dollar bills in that envelope," she said. "They are yours, whatever you decide to do as a result of listening to what I have to say. If you want more, tell me now, before I continue."

She waited and I shook my head, lazily.

"A century will be fine. If you are offering me a job there will also be expenses—if I take it. If I say no deal then you can keep your money. That is the way I do business. I might not get rich enough to get my name shouted out on Wall Street, but I feel clean when I look at my overdraft."

"I understand," she said. She came close to me again. "Last year Stanton got in with a very tough crowd. In no time at all they managed to fleece him of every last penny. I, of course, helped him to begin with. I lent him a substantial amount but before long he was at my door asking for more. I realized this was a situation that could only end in disaster, and tried to send him away but he made a dreadful scene and said he would kill himself if I didn't give him twenty thousand dollars. A gambling debt, he said. I stood firm and told him it was time he faced up to his responsibilities. He laughed in my face and said he would find the money another way.

"He did—by forging Father's signature on a number of stolen checks. He defrauded Father of a sum in the region of fifty thousand dollars. If this was not enough, the fraudulent checks then fell into the hands of a blackmailer who threatened to expose Stanton."

She paused to let the information sink in.

"No doubt the police can be persuaded not to press charges, but the shock would kill Father. Stanton is heir to half the family estate. He knows that the one thing that would make Father disinherit him would be the thought that his son was capable of acting in a way that could tarnish our name."

Elaine Damone's cute lisp was getting more pronounced. With a brother called Stanton it was having quite an airing.

"I couldn't let Father die because of his useless son. So I have been paying the blackmailer myself and have reimbursed Father's account from my own."

The grate in the fireplace was made up with some logs covered in crumbling bark. I flicked my cigarette into the back of the grate and finished my second highball.

While Elaine Damone had been talking, my eyes had wandered again to a large picture frame in the center of the mantelpiece. Two silver diamond-shaped pillars held glass panes on a base of white marble.

"You can guess what I am leading up to," she said. "Where this sordid business requires your involvement?"

"Sure," I said. "Forget what you read in *Black Mask* and *True Detective*, the stories about dicks turning up their noses at anything less than retrieving stolen jade from drug-crazed nymphomaniacs. Divorce and blackmail, in that order, that's what keeps the fleas jumping in my pants."

"I take it you will accept the case of ascertaining the identity and whereabouts of my brother's blackmailer?"

"That's right," I said. "And I'll try not to shed too many tears for your brother while I'm doing it. Now that I'm on the Damone payroll you'd better give me some details."

"Before I do that," Elaine Damone said, "I insist you work in strict accordance with my instructions. To ensure this, I will pay you one hundred dollars a day and a bonus of two thousand when—or should I say if—you unmask this felon."

Her voice now had the tone the rich use for addressing hirelings. I could hear old man Damone yelling about the place, balling out some half-witted Negro for not decanting the vintage claret and then serving it with the lobster.

"There is no if about it, lady," I said. "For two Gs I'll have your brother's blackmailer tarred and feathered in the marketplace."

"That is precisely what you will not do," she said sharply. "There can be no guarantee that the police will not prosecute Stanton. The faintest whiff of scandal would give the gossip-mongers just what they want. They would love an opportunity to sneer openly at our family. I have already explained the effect this would have on my father. Get this absolutely clear: I am paying you well for one reason, to ensure that whoever is blackmailing Stanton will never set foot in a police cell, a courtroom or anywhere else before he faces Damone justice. When he is located I want you to give me notification of who he is and where he is. Nothing more."

"And then some hired gun will take care of him?"

"That is none of your business. You will not be implicated in anything other than the duties I have outlined. You have my word, the word of a Damone, on that."

"Fine," I said. "Only you better keep Stanton in his playpen until this thing blows over."

She gave me one of her frosty smiles. "That has already been taken care of. I have organized a little tour of Europe, which he somewhat reluctantly accepted. Right now he is on a liner halfway across the Atlantic."

I thought about that. When I was last there the place was in rubble. Europe needed Stanton Damone like Valentino needed the talkies.

"Who does the blackmailer contact?" I asked. "You or your brother?"

"He obviously contacted Stanton to begin with. Then I decided it would be better for all concerned if I took over the responsibility and Stanton was kept as far away as possible."

"How many payments have there been?"

"Three, to the best of my knowledge. Each time he asks for more and always uses a different system." She paused. "It will not be easy to track him down."

Elaine Damone picked up the envelope and said, "Find Stanton's blackmailer and you will not find my gratitude wanting."

Then suddenly, startlingly, she parted her crimson lips, raised her mouth to mine and laid on the kind of kiss a woman gives when she wants to say, "Big strong man go hunt meat, chop down tree—and be quick about it."

It made me feel dizzy enough to faint into one of her box-shaped chairs. But I resisted. The last time I saw one like it was on death row. It had electric wires going into it and a lever in another room. Then Elaine Damone said, "What, in your professional opinion, is our next step?"

"We sit tight till he calls," I said, pulling a dog-eared calling card from my billfold. I handed it to her.

"The printed number gets me when I am not eating or sleeping. The other number is Charlie's Bar. I sleep in a room at the top of the building. The bar has a phone, but not my room. Charlie will take messages when I am not there, but he is not my secretary so treat him with respect."

She nodded and we both smiled. Elaine because she was pleased some nut was getting her family out of a jam. I smiled because I was born that way. Goofy.

16

In a quiet, sunlit avenue lined with elms I sidestepped a tubby man in brightly checked plus fours and brown shoes with what looked like snow on the caps, and flagged down the only cab in sight.

I flopped into the back and said, "Sherman Towers."

The cabby had coffee-colored skin and a droopy black mustache. He was a Zapata look-alike if ever I saw one.

I opened the window, lit a cigarette and threw the match out.

"Where you from?" I asked. "As a matter of interest."

"The South," he said. "If you call that interesting."

"Savannah?"

"South America, gringo."

"Why keep it a secret?"

"I don't speak the English so good."

"You speak it fine," I said. "Better than Popeye."

"Go—your sister," he spat, and overshot a red.

"You'll get yourself busted driving like that," I said. "This state is hot on wetbacks. They'll send you back to Peru."

"Brazil," he said softly.

"Isn't that where the coffee comes from? And copper?"

He said he wouldn't know about that.

"Sure it does," I said. "First gold, then sugar, then coffee, then copper." Without pausing I added, "Ever hear of the Damone family?"

"The name don't mean a thing."

"Think a bit. There's a son. Early twenties. Dark, I guess.

Probably a good-looking slob. Gambles. A wow with dames."

The back of his head shook and his shoulders shrugged. "Nope."

"Yeah," I said. "Everyone your side knows the Damones. The daughter is a real looker. Puts Ava Gardner in the shade. The Damones own your town and the town next to it. They own half where you come from."

"Like I say, the name don't mean a thing."

"You're kidding. I just been drinking with the daughter. You should see her place. Cost millions."

"Invite me along sometime."

"You got to see the place to believe it. It's got everything. Interior design isn't the word."

"Dandy," he said.

The cab pulled up to the curb outside Sherman Towers. Twenty-four hours after Norma Summers hit the sidewalk there was nothing to mark the horror. No marks, no rubber-necks, no police. It might never have happened. It was just another busy sidewalk on another busy day.

I paid the cabby.

"Let me tell you something odd," I said. "This Damone dame I told you about, the one with everything and more. There is one thing she doesn't have."

"Surprise me, gringo."

"On her mantelpiece there is a picture frame. But it doesn't have a picture."

His eyes narrowed. "So what else is new?" He drove off to look for a fare who just wanted to chew the fat.

"It's just damned odd," I shouted at the disappearing cab, and nearly stepped in front of a truck.

My Packard had a parking ticket on the windshield and someone had dented the rear bumper. Just the usual. I climbed in and drove home in no particular hurry.

It was lunchtime at Charlie's Bar. I squeezed through a small mob fighting amiably for food and a seat to consume it in, ordered something and sat down at a double table that was already occupied by an old Jew in a drab topcoat. He was simultaneously sucking soup noisily and reading the business page of the *Philadelphia Post*'s midday edition.

He didn't look up as I sat down. My lunch came in the shape of a grilled porterhouse steak and a bottle of Harper's Bonded Bourbon. I unscrewed the cap on the Harper's and filled a small tumbler to the brim.

"Here's to Old King Cole," I said for no reason I knew, and threw the liquid down my throat.

The Jew lowered his newspaper, gave me a short disapproving glare over a pair of half-rimmed spectacles and carried on reading. As I ate I let my eyes wander over his paper.

The front page was top-heavy with thick type and a four-column-wide, twelve-inch-deep photo of Harry S. Truman waving his hat in the air and smiling. There wasn't much about anything else, but what there was I read. Grace Sanderry's old man had got himself into one story. A short account, with a quote, about why his company was selling off twenty-five percent of its blue-chip investments. There was a weather report, a few lines about the stock market and a stop-press item next to the list of shows on WFIL radio. I leaned forward and read:

> TUG HAND FINDS DROWNED MAN
> At approximately 7:20 this morning tug hand Erik Jurgens found the body of a man floating in the Delaware. The man, whom police later named as Walter Kirkpatrick, 43, was discovered north of Red Bank as the tug *Topeka* was heading to her mooring down river.
>
> Mr. Kirkpatrick worked as an official for the Grand Union of Pennsylvania Insurance Company. A spokesman for the company said today that routine investigations into his business activities by senior executives may have had an unsettling effect.
>
> The police are considering suicide as the most probable . . .

Suddenly I wasn't looking at the newspaper anymore.

"You wanna buy a paper?" the Jew said. "Only one owner. Give me five cents and you can take it away."

I gave him a weak smile instead and drank some more of the liquor, straight. No ice, no soda, no diced fruit.

Then I thought a bit about the last two days. Mostly I thought about Elaine Damone driving around in the small hours looking fresh as a bunch of spring daffodils. I thought about how she dressed, how she walked, how she lisped, how she used her lips. I thought about her neater-than-neat ways, her hidden passion, her almond eyes and her wealth. Then I thought about the jam her brother had gotten into. And I liked thinking about all of that. Except maybe the bit about her no-good brother. It didn't add up. Elaine Damone was nobody's fool. She needed a Pinkerton man, not a down-at-heel dick like me. If she wanted discretion she could buy that on half what she was paying me. For a century a day, a Pinkerton dick with his type of back-up could have wound up the operation in less time than it takes to chew the sugar out of a Chiclet.

But I wasn't complaining. I poured out another Harper's and chalked it up to expenses.

Then I began thinking about Norma Summers and about her husband's killers. Then I went cold and my brow went clammy. Suddenly I wasn't feeling so pleased with myself. For the first time I realized what I thought I had got myself out of was still there. It was like waking up to an illness.

Hog and Frenchy were pros. That meant the racketeer who paid their salary would have been told of my involvement with Summers. The rumor that I knew the whereabouts of the briefcase would have certainly been passed on to the boss. He was probably still waiting for the three of us to show.

I didn't like what that added up to. But it made life interesting. I would have to track down a high-powered blackmailer while ducking and running from a high-powered mobster. No trouble for a man of my experience. I could handle it with no more than a few minor adjustments to my life. Like changing my name, growing a beard and wearing my socks inside out. Given time I could handle it fine. But how much time was there? How long was a piece of string? Who's Sorry Now? All good questions. All without answers.

I gulped some more bourbon.

At that very moment my waiting room was probably crammed full of hoods in all shapes and sizes, pointing pistols, smoking fat cigars and yelling for me to come out from behind the filing cabinet.

I poured out more drink and drank.

I picked up the half-empty bottle and said shalom to the Jew. One nostril quivered disapprovingly as he solemnly shook his head. He was aching to explain what a bottle of neat bourbon would do to me. I got up before he had the chance.

There was nobody in my office. Nobody at all. The rooms smelled damp and were heavy with the odor of stale tobacco. I picked up three letters from the mat and padded through Reception. There was a lot of dust and dirt I hadn't noticed. It looked like it had been there some time.

I pulled the string of the venetian blind as if I were running up a ship's flag and threw open the casement window. In the street, three floors below a dozen men stripped to their undershirts were drilling a hole in the asphalt. They weren't doing it so no one would notice.

I flopped into my wooden swivel chair, dragged my heels up onto the desk and opened the mail.

The top letter was a circular from a credit card company giving me ten reasons why I should become a subscriber. The letter was typed and finished off with a simulated hand-written signature, printed in the color of blue fountain pen ink. It was signed J.J. Klondurgle, or something like that.

The next envelope had a window and the look of a bill inside. I dropped it in the wastebasket, unopened, along with the circular.

I'd seen the writing on the third letter several times before. The pale lavender envelope had no stamp and had

"Delivered by hand" printed extra carefully in the top left-hand corner. It was from the twelve-year-old daughter of the building's janitor. Some time back I got her a puppy from somewhere and ever since she has written at least once a week, pledging her undying love. From time to time she puts a piece of candy in the envelope. Not this time. There was a lock of fair hair tied with pink ribbon. The envelope reeked of the perfume young girls buy. It costs five cents a bucket and they get through two buckets a day. The thing with the janitor's daughter was the nearest I had ever come to a permanent relationship.

I put her letter in a drawer and took the Harper's from my raincoat pocket. The half-full bottle felt good in my hand. It was a great comfort in times of stress. I tried worry beads once but they didn't taste so good.

I lit a cigarette and blew a lungful of smoke into the ozone. Stanton Damone's blackmailer was going to be a tough cookie to find, with or without his sister's kisses.

I extracted my .38 from my holster, a square of oily canvas and a can of gun grease from the desk drawer and took the gun apart. I laid the parts out in three neat rows. There were forty-seven separate pieces and I cleaned each one meticulously, thoroughly greasing all the parts that moved. I did it all in the time it took to finish the Harper's.

When I had screwed back the walnut stock to the nickel frame, I opened a fresh pack of shells and slipped six into the chamber. I checked along the two-inch barrel with its left twist rifling and then held the weapon at arm's length. I closed one eye, and without releasing the safety catch squeezed the trigger. It all felt fine. It had to be. It was my life insurance.

I put the gun in its holster and the cloth and cleaning stuff back in the drawer. It was time I did something about the mug who had lost his briefcase. I knew two people who might help.

Captain Bananier was an old cop who knew every punk from Philly to Miami and he always gave a shamus with a war record an even break. He had a line on everyone, from the

Sicilians with pea-shooters to the small-time rats who stole each other's fleas.

I called his office and was told he was out of town.

That left me with a news hawk by the name of Harvey Hendersson.

I dialed the *Philadelphia Post* and asked for Crime.

17

On the way to the *Post* I stopped off at Tardelli's for a shave and a haircut. With the stubble gone, I did up my shirt and wound the tie Elaine Damone gave me round my neck. It would have looked great on Gary Cooper or Alan Ladd or Donald Duck. It didn't look great on me. I took it off and gave it to Tardelli. I then walked a block and a half before I found the kind of store that sold the kind of tie I enjoyed tying. I found it on Hoffman. The window was dressed with dead flies and some chrome stands piled high with yellowing detachable collars, boxes of tarnished cufflinks and a whole heap of cheap accessories.

Ten minutes later I walked out wearing a yard of maroon imitation satin with a painting of a bare-breasted Hawaiian dancer in a grass skirt on the front.

Elaine Damone would understand.

The *Post* was on Broad Street, a ten-story brick building as architecturally undistinguished as the eight miles of buildings on either side. Broad Street may have been the longest straight road in the world. It was certainly the dullest.

A large truck filled a narrow side street adjoining the *Post* building. It was piled high with rolls of virgin newsprint that looked like overgrown reels of white cotton thread. Two massive Negroes with coal black skin were climbing over the rolls of paper, winching them on a hoist from the truck and down through an opening in the sidewalk to the print room below street level. A light rain had begun to fall. It washed over their faces making their skin shine like it had been coated with varnish. The taller of the two spat on his hands and pulled the zipper of his tartan mackinaw right up to his neck. Then he pushed the loaded winch effortlessly away from his body and started singing something I had never heard before.

Dusk fell quickly. Around me, in the high buildings, office lights flickered on, one after the other in quick succession. They lit up the sky like tracer bullets.

I climbed three steps, pushed through a swinging door and walked up to the *Post* security guard who stood behind a long desk. I told him I was expected, flashed my license and waited while he called. Then he spoke my name once and nodded twice.

"Reception says to go up," he said. "The City Room is on five."

I said I knew the way and strolled to the bank of automatic elevators.

I lit a cigarette and blew smoke at the oil painting of the *Post*'s founder. He was trying not to be strangled by a high wing collar and glared out from the canvas with steel gray eyes. The artist had squeezed a lot of paint trying to give the old bird a look of integrity, but succeeded only in making Gaynor J. Covey look mean and cruel. But I doubt if he had noticed and he certainly liked the picture enough to let it hang smack in the middle of the lobby. He may have even liked it enough to have paid for it.

The doors opened and I squeezed into the elevator with a small crowd.

The receptionist on the City floor was one I hadn't seen before. She was a forbidding middle-aged number with dumpy arms and a hairy chin.

She looked for a long time at my tie before saying anything.

Then she said, "Yes?"

"I've got an appointment with Harvey Hendersson," I said. "He's expecting me."

She tried a polite smile and missed. By a mile. "Your name?" she said, like she expected me to say I hadn't got one.

"Mike Dime," I growled. "The guy downstairs told you I was coming up."

She was sitting behind a prim desk with a small potted cactus to her right, a PBX to her left, and in front of her a list of personnel and their extension numbers.

"I'll just see if Mr. Hendersson is free," she chimed, running the sharpened point of a fingernail laboriously down the rows of numbers.

"It's extension 346," I said. "And by the way, what happened to the pretty little strawberry blonde who used to have this job?"

She didn't reply. Just read down the typed list until she found the number for herself. Then she dialed three times and with her gaze fixed on the ceiling described a man in a raincoat, tattered hat and a loud tie. She said that this man claimed he had an appointment. She said all this like a witness in a rape trial. She then said my name.

Harvey Hendersson said something I couldn't hear and the smirk went clean off her face. She took the instrument from her ear and looked at it as if it had just bitten her.

"Really, Mr. Hendersson," she snapped indignantly. "That is no way to address a lady."

I could hear his laughter at the other end.

I pushed my way through two heavy glass swinging doors faced with polished copper and walked into the City Room. It was vast and brightly lit and dominated by a large horseshoe of desks. Several dozen men in shirtsleeves were frantically clacking typewriters and talking into telephones. They looked jaded. There had been three election specials, and they had got it wrong as could be.

I went behind a row of copy editors pushing their blue pencils rapidly and confidently across sheet after sheet of paper black with words. Every desk was covered by a maze of phones, pads, photos, beer bottles, cups, ashtrays, cigarette packs, erasers, pencils, food, address books, phone directories, cuttings from other editions, other newspapers, magazines, carbon paper and paper clips. Now and then there was a story.

The typewriters clattered on like an army of chipmunks with metal teeth.

A man with white hair and a crimson nose the shape of an onion was leaning back in his chair. His hands were linked over his domed belly and his eyes were shut tight. The sheet of white paper curled under the roller of his old Remington was blank as a parson's dog collar. A lightweight gray jacket was draped over the back of his chair. One pocket was almost touching the floor, the silver neck of a hip flask just visible.

The man at the next desk was talking softly into a phone. He sounded deeply concerned. He was asking someone to explain exactly what happened when the husband came home and found the blue sock that wasn't his in the shower.

I pushed my way through and stopped outside a door with the name Harvey Hendersson painted in a bold sans serif face on the frosted glass panel. Hendersson had been given the supreme accolade in journalism: an office to himself.

"Don't bother knocking, Dime, old buddy. It's open," the man behind the door shouted. His voice was as enthusiastic as any top crime man's had the right to be.

I entered the office and was greeted with a vigorous handshake that sent my arm up and down like the handle of a water pump.

The man doing the pumping topped six feet by three inches or more and carried around a hundred and fifty pounds on a springy frame. He observed the world through horn-rimmed glasses that had a hairline crack running through the left lens. The right temple bar was held together with adhesive tape. His flaxen hair had a side part that was too low and a fringe that overhung his brow like a thatch. His cheeks wore a healthy tan and his chin jutted out as if it were offering an invitation to an uppercut. The last guy who accepted the invitation needed a team of interns to put back the pieces.

"Well, well, old pal," he said, as I eased myself gently into the visitor's seat. "What's on your mind?"

Hendersson stepped from behind his desk and perched himself on the window ledge. He thrust his hands deep into his trouser pockets and waited for me to say something.

I told him what I had told Elaine Damone the night she picked me up, about the case of dough, about Hog and the

French kid and about Norma and Frank. I told him I thought I was fingered and needed to know who was doing the fingering. I told him I needed to know because I had another case and I would be letting my client down if I turned up for work with a bullet in my head. I didn't say too much about Elaine. She was a chapter on her own.

Hendersson heard me with a thoughtful expression on his face, ignoring the phone on his desk, which rang incessantly.

Only when I had finished talking did he flop back into his chair and finally pick up the phone. His bright face turned more and more weary as the party on the other end of the line made a long speech. Now and then Harvey said "Yes, honey," but mostly he said nothing. As he listened, his eyes wandered fondly along the rows of books that lined every inch of wall. There were books about people who committed crimes, wanted to commit crimes, regretted having committed crimes. There were books on the people who caught criminals and the people who sentenced them. A lot of the books had the name Harvey Hendersson running up the spine.

Finally the crime hound scribbled something quickly on a foolscap pad and hung up. He let out a long, low whistle.

"Mrs. Hendersson," he said apologetically. "There has been a great tragedy in the Hendersson home. We are having a dinner party and my wife left the ice cream to melt on the front seat of the station wagon."

I smiled the smile of the gratefully unmarried.

"Give me a lead," I said, "and I'll replace it."

"The station wagon?"

"The ice cream."

Hendersson unloosened his shirt collar and pulled down his tie and laughed. He got up from the desk, sauntered to the door and stuck his head out.

"Two black coffees, fast," he shouted and went back to his chair.

"I can give you Hog and his buddy," he said, picking up a yellow pencil and tapping the end rhythmically on the desk.

"Those two torpedoes have been on the scene some time. They're nothing classy, but definitely not small-time."

"They *were*," I corrected him.

The door opened and a leggy redhead rumba-ed in carrying two cups of coffee on the lid of a cardboard box.

She gave Harvey a dizzy smile and put the cups on his desk. She did this by holding the rims delicately between her thumb and middle finger. Her nails had bright red polish on them. She was in a skin-tight skirt and a black and white polka dot blouse with padded shoulders.

"I couldn't find the tray, Mr. Hendersson," she said, opening her big green-gray eyes wider than Texas. "I looked everywhere."

"Forget it, Miss Spivac," Harvey said absently and started to stir sugar into his cup with the eraser end of his yellow pencil.

"Oh, Mr. Hendersson!" The redhead gave the air a downward slap with an open palm. "You said you were gonna quit calling me Miss Spivac and call me by my first name."

She looked over her shoulder and winked at me. "It's Shirley. Pretty, don't you think?"

"That's not all," I said. She laughed openly, picked up the makeshift tray and rumba-ed out.

Harvey sipped his coffee and leaned back in his chair. He waited for me to cool down and then started to talk.

"The way I see it, the key to your problem is to be found in the origin of the cash in the briefcase. I can tell you that there have been no thefts of sums in that amount for some time, and none that we have been forced to suppress. You and I both know there are times when editors are under pressure to spike stories not considered in the public interest. All that means is the big boys have got cold feet. And that kind of thing always happens at election time. A clean crime sheet, even a phony one, gives the mayor and governor and all the rest of the gang a warm feeling and a lot of votes. In my view the money here is illegitimate. You might say that a lot of straight organizations occasionally have tax problems that are solved by cash transactions, but they would never use a pair of out-of-town robots like your boys to do their work."

"Could it be mob warfare?" I asked, got up, fetched my coffee and sat down.

"This isn't Chicago, Dime. Philly hasn't got mobs."

Hendersson took a pipe from a long rack of about twenty pipes hidden under an untidy pile of papers. He looked at it for a moment and then bit on the vulcanite mouthpiece.

"I've got a hunch that a story I've been vaguely following might—I emphasize, just *might*—throw a little light on the matter."

"Tell me," I said. "It's dark as a tomb where I'm sitting."

He took the pipe from his mouth.

"Did you by any chance read about the insurance stiff who made an inch on the front page of our midday edition?" His free hand rummaged through the papers. "There's a copy around here someplace."

"I read it," I said. "Some guy called Kirkpatrick. They pulled him out of the river."

"The cops are stuck. On the surface, the late Walter Kirkpatrick was as straight as the Appian Way. But what the cops don't know is that he is the eighth insurance agent in as many states to die in unaccountable circumstances."

"Insurance agents have got to die sometime," I said.

Harvey Hendersson got up, pulled a file drawer open and flipped over the contents. He extracted a blue folder and handed it to me.

"Look for yourself. The subject is insurance men dying suddenly during the last three years. Jack Prescott, in December forty-five. Hanged himself in the state of Colorado. George Chesliegh of Phoenix, Arizona, supposedly fell off a ladder while fixing a roof leak. That was July of last year. Victor Goldmark, another drowned man in New York State. And so the list goes on. What I am saying, Dime, is that there is a clearly identifiable pattern that links these apparently unconnected deaths."

I put the file on the floor next to my chair, along with my empty coffee cup. Hendersson said, "Did you ever hear of a prewar trickster called Manny Gluck? At least, that was the name on his death certificate." A finger jabbed at the bridge of his specs.

I shook my head. "You know me, Harvey. I pickled my memory long ago. The only reason I have cards printed is so I'm sure to find my way home."

Hendersson put the briar pipe back between his teeth and tried to get it to burn from a ceramic bust of Abraham Lincoln, which doubled as a desk lighter. He sucked hard three or four times, lost the flame and ran out of patience. He threw the lighter down and put the pipe in the Out box.

"Manny Gluck was small-time beans," he said. "Until he stumbled on an insurance racket that was damn near perfect. The operation was beautifully simple. The scheme was based on nothing more than turning up an insurance agent with an eye for the extra buck and only the slimmest chances of getting it through promotion, the way most do. It didn't even need a big capital outlay. Gluck simply offered to purchase long-term insurance policies—the longer they had to run the better—and hand the agent a fifty-fifty partnership in a mutual company formed with the stuff from under the counter. The agent would duplicate the original policy, but transfer the cash to his and Gluck's new company. All assets were kept liquid and it was, on the surface, no more serious a crime than stealing someone else's business. I suppose there was a slight criminal risk for the agent, but only slight, and that could be easily explained away by a sharp mouthpiece. Gluck's genius was in picking agents who were ripe for that kind of caper. The perfect qualifications would be a weakness for fast dough and a streak of disloyalty. Men of that ilk don't usually find their way into executive jobs in large and profitable insurance companies. But they do come along now and again. When they did, Manny Gluck was waiting. He had the news hound's nose for the tip-off and an evangelist's sweet talk. But to protect himself, once the agent was sold on the scheme,

Gluck put in a front man. In the event of a policy being realized before it matured, the company would be wound up at once. It was the front man's job to burn the books and company stationery and all the other phony papers and to assist the agent with his getaway to Mexico or somewhere out of reach of state and federal laws. At least, that would have been the story."

"But in reality it was down to the St. James Infirmary? The old city morgue?"

"Right," Hendersson said. "A convincing suicide, leaving the authorities thinking the whole thing was a one-shot deal by a greedy first-timer who went and lost his nerve."

"If it was so perfect," I said, "how did you get to hear about it?"

Hendersson laughed.

"Gluck picked an agent who had thought of much the same game, but obviously he could never work it. When Gluck came along, he allowed himself to be suckered. As soon as the lights were red, he bumped off the front man, tipped off the cops about Manny and took the first banana boat to Rio. Along with the cash."

"The insurance men you just showed me," I said. "Are they part of a similar racket?"

"I'd bet on it. The briefcase must have contained the hard assets of the operation, with Kirkpatrick as the fall guy. It fits, Dime, it fits beautifully." He smiled a big, happy smile. "The question we ask now is this. Has someone worked out this operation for himself or did Manny Gluck leave the blueprint in his will? Find the answer and you find the man who lost his briefcase in the john of the Three Sixes. Of that I am certain. But I must remind you that any information you dig up is high risk. Explosive. Everyone will want a piece. The cops, the hoods, the insurance company, everyone. I will even want a little myself. You will be in deep, Dime. And it will be damn hot."

I shook my head.

"Don't worry about me, Harvey. There hasn't been a day since I was born that someone hasn't tried to throw me back. Tell me one more thing. Where did Manny Gluck do his time?"

"Up river, Ossining Correctional Facility. Sing Sing to you."

I stuck out a hand and let Harvey Hendersson jerk it up and down again.

"Ever hear of Stanton Damone?" I asked as I was about to close the office door. "Somebody local is blackmailing him."

"Get out of here," Harvey Hendersson said, selecting a meerschaum pipe with an amber tip from the rack. "You've wasted enough of my time already."

He scribbled something on his pad. It could have been a name, a name like Stanton Damone. Or Singapore Sadie, or anything.

"Call me in a day," he said. Then the phone rang and his mind moved on.

Outside, a deep purple night was about to pick a fight with itself. Black clouds sparred in an electric sky, throwing thunder in sudden combinations.

I got in my car and crawled back to the office in a long line of red and yellow lights. By the time I had parked and switched on the lights in my office, rain was falling cold and steady.

18

The phone was ringing impatiently as I strolled through the outer office. I unbuttoned my raincoat, one button at a time, hung it on the bentwood coat rack, took off my battered hat, placed it on the larger of the two hooks, sat down at my desk, twiddled the wooden nipples on my day-by-day desk calendar, brought myself up to date, lit a cigarette and threw the match into an ashtray. Then I picked up the receiver.

"Dime," I said politely. "At your service."

It was Elaine Damone.

"Where in heaven's name have you been?" she said stiffly. "I have been calling both the numbers you gave me I don't know how many times."

"I hope you weren't rude to Charlie."

"There was no need. He has better manners than you."

I blew some smoke into the phone.

"If you have not forgotten, Mr. Dime, you have accepted a commission on behalf of a member of my family. It might be of some interest to you that Stanton's blackmailer has made contact."

I said I hadn't forgotten.

"I am delighted to hear it," she said. "He will be letting me know the exact details of the drop, as he calls it, sometime tomorrow. In the meantime I am to get three thousand dollars in used bills and make myself available at a minute's notice. It could be any time of the day or night."

As she finished her speech a doorbell chimed faintly in the background. But she did not answer it. Nor did the maid. I heard it chime again.

"Once again, I must repeat that I want only the identity of this creature. He has made it abundantly clear that if he is challenged in any way, the forged checks will be dispatched to my father without argument. Please remember, no funny business. Get any ideas of being some sort of hero right out of your sometimes less than clear head. And try to stay sober."

"Listen," I said, stabbing my cigarette into the ashtray. It was time I put Elaine Damone straight. "I like working for you because I like what you pay and when your icy smile melts you look lovely. You look lovely when you don't smile. I like your swinging hips, your rounded earlobes, your little-girl lisp, your taste in handbags and your way of dealing with over-attentive gas station attendants. I even like pink silk sheets. I can only imagine how you would make whoopee, but I guess I'd like that too. But there is something I don't like. I am not crazy about being told how to do my job. It may not have occurred to you but I am in a tough profession. I put my life on the line every time I go snooping into someone else's private life. Some people get sensitive about it, especially blackmailers. A dick tapping their line can make them turn real nasty, *muy enojado*, as they say south of the border. Something else you should hear about blackmailers: they love making threats. They live by them. Sometimes they carry them out. And the best are always one step ahead of the game. They can spot a tail faster than a lizard's tongue grabs flies. Once I am in the open I have to play it my way. Otherwise there is a risk that everyone will get their lungs permanently emptied of air and their very last photograph taken by the police department. Then, I guess if you are you, you will get a long obituary in *Time* magazine. But if you are me, you just get the janitor's daughter wasting her pocket money on a bunch of flowers. It's as simple as that."

She understood it all, except for the bit about the janitor's daughter. But it didn't make any difference. I didn't think it would.

"You will do it my way," she said calmly. "Or not at all."

There was a long pause while I calmed down.

"Okay," I said. "Forget I puffed out my feathers. It's just that some days I feel like a lump of chewed mutton."

Neither of us knew what I meant by that so we each said a perfunctory good-bye and hung up.

The receiver of the phone was still warm when I picked it up once more. It was time I ran up a few cents on my unpaid phone bill.

First I called downtown and asked who, if anyone, was looking into why Kirkpatrick should want to jump in the Delaware. I got put through to the desk sergeant who said that he didn't think anyone was, but if I phoned in the morning someone else would know. I said that I needed to know now and he asked who wanted to know and I said I had some information that whoever was dealing with the matter would like to hear about. He then put me onto someone else who put me onto someone or another who told me that a Detective Noonan was on the case but that he had gone home. I thanked whoever it was and hung up.

I then called the operator and asked her to get me Sing Sing, and had her connect me with Prison Liaison. After a few clicks and buzzes and the same rigmarole that I had at police HQ, a voice chewing energetically on a lump of gum said, "What can I do for you, bud?"

Men who work in state penitentiaries hate private investigators almost as much as they hate convicts. Hating people comes with the job, along with the free uniform, annual leave and the occasional knife in the ribs.

"Detective Noonan speaking," I barked, rolling my words rapidly, one into the other. I didn't want to sound too likable or intelligent. That would have blown my cover faster than a fish drinks water.

"Philly Police. Who am I talking to? What's that? Speak up."

"Er . . . er . . . Gorsey . . ."

"Sir," I shouted. "Gorsey, *sir*. Always address a senior ranking officer as sir. Got that, Gorsey? Now listen carefully. This is top priority. I require information most urgently on the prison record of a former inmate named Manny, or Emmanuel Gluck. Gluck is spelled G for George, L for Lisbon, U for Uncle, C for Charlie, K for Kansas. Got that? The period in question is prewar, and as I understand, this Gluck character may have died before terminating his sentence. Is that clear? Now here's the deal. I want a list of all inmates who may have shared Gluck's cell. I know it's a tall order and I realize that it's late and that the record office is probably closed. So it should be. But, I stress, this information is classified A.I. Crucial. It is required to help crack a case of international proportions. It couldn't be tighter. We go in tonight or never. Got that? Now get this. If we come up with the goods, the police commissioner has promised promotion down the line to any officer who it was found acted beyond the normal course of duty. How old are you, Gorsey?"

"Twenty-three, sir."

"You get my drift?"

"Yes, sir."

"Then get to it, boy."

"Yes, sir."

I said I would call back in an hour and put the receiver on its hook. I took out the photograph I'd found on Frenchy's cadaver, turned it over and had another squint at the number scrawled on the back. For a reason I couldn't pin down, it interested me more than the people. As I read the number again and again, a face strained to be seen behind a mist of memories. It was telling me a familiar name, but not so loud that I could hear. As the face appeared and took a shape, so it vanished once more. Like a bird when it flies across the sun. I looked at my watch. It said a little after eight. I picked up the phone, dialed the operator and read out the number. I asked for the name of the subscriber and his or her address. The voice at the other end said she would call me back. I looked at my watch again. It said a little more after eight. I was doing fine.

To kill an hour, I emptied out a few drawers and threw a pile of old papers into the wastebasket. Then I placed a sheet of newspaper over the pool of rainwater under the window and sat down and looked some more at the people in the photo. I thought that it was odd for a hood to carry such a picture. The doll was a looker but no Betty Grable. Apart from the fact that I wouldn't like to meet her pal with the hard eyes, I didn't make it add up to much.

When I got back to Sing Sing, Gorsey had gone off duty. But he had left a full list, his rank, number, phone number, home address, birthplace and zodiac sign. If there was a promotion coming, Gorsey wasn't going to be forgotten.

I copied down a list of ten names. Only two cell mates had survived Gluck, who had died, aged 67, in jail while serving two terms of seven to fourteen years for fraud and conspiracy to murder. The men who survived him were Angelo Mellinski and Warren Ratenner. Mellinski shared a cell with Gluck for less than a year. But Ratenner seemed promising. He scratched around with Gluck for nearly three years and was Gluck's cell mate at the time of his death. Ratenner did seven years for fraud and tax evasion. He was released in 1945.

I called the *Post* and left a message about what I found with Miss Spivac, only I didn't call her that. I called her Shirley.

I made a squashed circle around Ratenner's name with my pencil and started to wonder why I was still alive and kicking. It made no difference whether the man who lost his briefcase was Warren Ratenner or the king of Siam. He knew where I hung out. I was in the book. Finding me was easy as pie. Easier. I should be picking lead out of my kneecaps but it was more peaceful around my office than in the reading room of a public library. What is more, he must have known that his hired stooges had messed things up. Forty-eight hours was too long a time for him to think they were still on their way, unless he was operating from a shack in Nova Scotia. Maybe he thought all three of us were double-crossing him. The Dime gang, with Hog and Frenchy. ACE GRIFTERS OUTSMART TOP MOBSTER. Read all about it.

Then the phone rang.

The address of the number on Frenchy's photo was on Porter Street and the name of the subscriber was a Mr. Max Slovan. Max Slovan. Yes, I knew Max.

Max Slovan's Poolroom was in the basement of a large furniture warehouse that Slovan leased from a Polish circus artist called the Great Waldo. Waldo had gone back to Poland just after the Depression and no one had heard of him since.

Slovan was in his fifties, or sixties, or seventies. No one knew. He had looked the same for as long as anyone could remember.

I walked down a short flight of steps, through a swinging door that had lost its swing and into a dark room hotter than a ship's stoke-hole. A maze of thick pipes threaded their way along the long, low ceiling, most of them carrying hot water. The skin of men who played in Slovan's regularly took on the bloodless pallor of old colonial Englishmen. Two rows of eight tables lined the vast basement. Silent pairs of players were bending, crouching or casually walking around the brightly lit oblongs of green baize, their faces solid with concentration, like surgeons operating, or priests celebrating mass. The subtropical room was thick with bluish gray tobacco smoke and extraordinarily quiet, except for the continual click of ivory balls. Now and again there was a sharp shout of disgust at an easy shot missed, or a yelp of surprise as a difficult shot was pocketed. But the rule of silence was a powerful feature of Max Slovan's Poolroom, an indication of how seriously he took the game.

I found him behind the counter where he kept a sleepy eye on the games and served lousy coffee and eats, which mostly consisted of cold, tasteless hot dogs that came with damp onions and mustard made from TNT. But you didn't go to Max Slovan's for the menu. You went to shoot pool.

He was sitting on a high stool cleaning his nails with a small file that he normally used to rub smooth the new tips on cues. He was tall, broad and heavy in a black shirt open at the neck. His trousers were light gray seersucker and belted by a thin strip of leather with a shiny gold-plated buckle. His face was moon-shaped, with a pair of huge dark eyebrows that grew out of his slim nose like the arched, jagged leaves of a palm tree. His thick black hair was parted in the center and slicked back in two almost solid sheaves. The track of the comb through the hair had left a straight, neat row of grooves, like rake marks on wet tar. His brow was as deeply furrowed as a field in winter. It all gave him the expression of a permanently worried man. Years back, when he shot pool as a professional, they called him Worrying Max Slovan, but they were wrong. He didn't have a worry in the world.

"Looking for a game?" Slovan said gently, like a doctor inquiring after your health. "I still got your stick somewhere. It's a nice piece of wood. Pity it don't get used much."

I pulled out a fresh pack of cigarettes, handed one to Max, who balanced it delicately behind his big ear. I tapped one against my bottom lip and lit it. "I hear all you shoot these days is people," he went on.

On the counter in front of him was a time clock with Roman numerals and a ticket for each game. Players paid by the hour. Two men came up to the counter putting on their jackets. They handed in their cues and paid and left without a word. Max rang up the change and closed the tray of the cash register with an easy push.

"You could have been useful if you had stuck at it," Slovan said, mournfully.

"There were too many better," I said. "Give me a cup of that stuff you call coffee and stop making me feel like the prodigal son. You know as well as I do that there are guys around this hall who can pocket a table full of balls with a bread stick and one hand tied behind their back. You could do it yourself."

Slovan grinned. "Easy, stranger," he said, pouring muddy liquid from a sweating copper urn.

I gave him some coins and he sat back on his stool.

"You haven't come for the coffee," he said. "And you haven't come here to shoot pool."

"Right," I said. "Both times."

Someone at the back of the room let out an overly loud "yippee" and Slovan hissed like the steam pipe of a locomotive. "Keep the noise down, you guys. Other guys is trying to concentrate."

The room went very quiet. Even the innocent chatter of the balls stopped for a second. "Nobody ever won a game of pool with their larynx," he said.

I took out the photo, told him about the number on the back and let him study it for a while. "Those faces mean anything to you?" I said. He rubbed his chin with a placid hand and made a wave ripple through the deeply etched rows of lines in his forehead. The furrows accentuated his concentration. He looked like he had been asked to explain the meaning of the universe.

Slovan shook his head. "You know this place. We get a lot of guys passing through. They come here and win a buck, lose a buck, then move on. I don't know them and don't want to know them. All I want is that they should play with their jaws closed tight and have enough loose change at the end of a frame to pay for the table. Regulars I got also, but the male mug in this pic ain't one of them. The guys I remember is the guys that stand the right way when they cue. If they pot good I remember them. Not otherwise. I never seen the dame either."

There was a chipped red fire bucket filled with sand hanging from the wall by Slovan's elbow. He turned his head and spat into it.

"Maybe someone else would remember if they saw this man playing here?" I said, and nodded at the spotlighted tables.

"Maybe," he said. "You could ask the guy in the corner, table sixteen." Max Slovan pointed to a solitary figure moving with great difficulty around the table. His legs were stiff as he walked and he took his body weight on his arms, using his cue and the rim of the table for crutches. Max said, "He can remember every angle on the table and every shot he ever played. Beats me how. Brain like a machine. A memory like I don't know what."

"Maybe it works with faces," I said, and left Max Slovan sitting on his stool, ponderously cleaning his nails.

In the far corner of the room, the frail-looking young man was bending awkwardly from the waist. His left forearm rested lightly on the baize, his bridge hand frozen into a solid claw. His legs were perfectly still, as if they were rooted to the ground. His cue arm moved smoothly backwards and forwards, sizing up the white ball, and then the man played his shot. The cue ball sent the eight ball thumping into a corner pocket before hovering almost imperceptibly on the point of contact and then spinning backwards the length of the table, as if fixed to the cue tip with an invisible elastic thread.

"One hell of a trick," I said as the player stood upright. "The name's Mike Dime." I put out a hand.

"I know," he said. "We met before. Only I knew you as Sarge." He moved nearer the bright lights over the table, took the black ball in his thin white hand and put it on its spot. "There's no reason why you should remember me, though. There were lots of guys like me, fresh-faced and greener than mint. Some you remember easy, like the big happy-go-lucky characters. Me, I have always been on the outside and kind of quiet."

He said all that without the slightest trace of bitterness. Obviously truth was one thing he wasn't afraid of. He held out his hand.

"Joey Pozo," he said. "Private Pozo of the Rangers, as was. We last met in France. June '45."

Then it came back. The stink of burning rubber, machines, oil, sometimes men. The incongruous summer breeze and salt drying on the skin. We shouted at each other to dig in but on that bright June morning there was no time. No time to dig, not even a handful of sand. Wave after wave of young men leaped from their landing craft into the shallow waters of the English Channel. The ones that made it to the beach crawled their way through the wreckage, shell holes and still-warm corpses. They kept flat to the earth as the noses of German guns poked through cement walls, their shells filling the air like a plague of locusts. The figures for June 6, 1944, say 3,283 men died and 12,000 were wounded. But there are other ways of dying, of being wounded that don't make the record books. They don't because no one knows how to tell it. A million men landed on Omaha and Sword and Utah and the other places. And it was one big death. Even for the guys who made it up the beach. Guys like Ranger Michael Dime of the First Army, Supreme Allied Expeditionary Force . . .

"What's up, Sarge?" someone was saying a long way off.

. . . He was nineteen years old and they found him sprawled on top of a man twice his age. They took off both Joey Pozo's legs in the field hospital and left him for dead. Someone took the trouble to count the number of bullet holes in the legs they threw away. There were forty-one. The army is an easy place to lose track of people in wartime, even a man with no legs.

"Hey, Sarge," the voice said again, a little nearer. "This is Slovan's. The war is over."

Joey Pozo was looking at me with his blue eyes wide open and his thin face pale and bewildered.

I was shaking uncontrollably and sweat was running off me like water from a shower nozzle. My hands were clammy and my throat thick and dry.

"You can put your gun away," Joey Pozo said. "The only Germans around here have never been east of Manhattan."

I was gripping my Detective Special tighter than a vice and pointing it all over the place. I ran the tip of my tongue over my lips and tasted the salt. I put the gun away and tried to say something. That something was, "What did they give you to walk on, soldier?"

Joey Pozo looked at me with his large, sad eyes, like those of a loris. There were dark lines coming from his nose, and dark lines grew from the corners of his thin lips. His hair was no color at all, just a reflection of the lights hanging over the table. Maybe it was a halo. It should have been. His mouth broke into a smile as he told me that his legs were cobbled together from tin, bits of wood and leather straps. He said they were okay for getting around a pool table but didn't do a lot for him in swimming trunks on the beach at Coney Island.

He told me that as a pool player having tin legs helped more than hindered. He told me that most players miss shots because their bodies move involuntarily at the moment they strike the cue ball. Playing a shot at pool is like firing a rifle: the slightest tremble sends the bullet off target. Pool players have the same problem. Joey Pozo told me that his problem was moving, not keeping stationary. With tin legs, he did that as naturally as Rockefeller earned interest.

"When I bend over," Pozo said, "my legs lock stiff. I'm as steady as a barrel of cement."

To demonstrate, he flicked the tip of his cue with a cube of sky blue chalk and set up the black ball six inches from the top left-hand pocket, an inch from the top cushion. He fished for the white ball with the end of his cue and placed it in the same position as the eight ball at the corresponding balk-end cushion.

"Once I got the angle," he said, "I'm so solid I can play this shot blindfolded." With the ease and confidence of a craftsman, Joey Pozo cracked the object ball firmly into the empty gap at the end of the baize. It hit the leather covering the brass pocket rim with a sharp crack that sounded like the explosion of a small-caliber pistol.

Joey Pozo looked at me and winked.

"Another thing," he said. "Tin don't get tired. I can do that all night long. And in this game sometimes you have to."

We talked some more, quietly so we didn't bother anyone playing, and I told Joey Pozo about the photo. He, like Max, had never seen the man or the woman. I mentioned the names of Mellinski and Ratenner. Neither name meant a thing. Then I got lucky. I explained how I got the photo and described Hog and Frenchy the way I last saw them.

Pozo's face brightened.

"The French guy I can give you," he said. "I took him for three hundred bucks about a week ago. Said he was new around Philly, asked if I knew any red lights, that sort of thing. He played pretty well for a man with a lot of lip. But he was wearing a different tie from the one you said. It was full of loud colors in a kind of zig-zag pattern. Like he'd spilled a fruit cocktail down his shirt. By the way, the shirt was different too." They were the details a man with a remarkable memory would remember. Or any woman.

"Anything else I could use?" I had been parked on the edge of a small table put there for drinks and ashtrays and all the bits and pieces players kept around. I got off and handed out some tobacco.

We both lit up and puffed a bit. Then Joey said, "Apart from telling me what a swell guy he was and how he beat some hot-shot pool player back in New York and some other whiz kid in New Orleans, he kept *molto sotto voce* about the kind of thing you want to hear."

I said I imagined he would have.

"But," Joey Pozo said, "the night I played him was not the last time I saw him."

"How was that?"

"He dropped in a night or two back and spent a long time on the pay phone." Joey pointed his cue into the gloom to a phone that was hanging on a low partition you could see over if you stood on tiptoe. Behind the partition a few crap tables were set aside for regulars. I looked over and saw one dark table and one brightly lit table in action. A bunch of zombies were mumbling numbers and slapping cards down onto the dull green cloth with sharp, agitated movements of their hands, as if they were shaking off surplus water before drying them.

"What night, exactly?" I said, picking up a cue from the rack and rolling it idly over the bed of the pool table, testing it for straightness.

Joey thought carefully for a second. "Election night, it must have been," he said. "The place was sort of on the empty side. I remember. This Frenchy guy comes running in here like he had a bounty hunter on his tail. He says nothing but goes right to the phone and starts shoving coins in the slot like it was a fruit machine."

"Hear a name?" I said, and put the cue back in the rack. It was crooked enough to be mayor of Chicago.

"Names, no. At least, not complete names. There was maybe a Dutch, and maybe a Larry or Harry. But I wasn't close to him and I wasn't paying attention."

Joey said he would keep his eyes and ears open and I left him my card and a few bucks.

I climbed back into the night and took in a lungful of cold, fresh air. I kept it down for a minute and blew it out slow. I did it again. It tasted better with smoke. Then I got into my car, drove east for two blocks and noticed something I should have thought of earlier. The Three Sixes was a block and a half from Max's. It was a ten minute walk.

Someone running fast could have done it in less than half that.

20

I was driving nowhere in particular, having decided I was safe as long as I kept moving. Avoiding my regular haunts would make me a lot harder to find and a lot harder to hit.

It was late now. Later than midnight and my head was begging to be let go and lie down someplace, and my arms and legs and the other parts joined in. I opened the car window and pinched my temples between a thumb and index finger while resting my elbow on the door. I sighed deeply and made some silly noises with my lips, like a horse neighing. None of that made me feel better. Sleep was what I needed. Days and nights of it.

I took a pack of Camels one-handed and lit one ditto. I eased up on the gas pedal and settled down for a long night cruising the streets of Philadelphia. Maybe one day I would write a book about it. *My Night of Adventure in America's Birthplace*. It would be the shortest book ever written.

I crawled onto Broad Street and kept heading north. I looked into the rearview mirror to see if I had a tail. At the speed I was going it would be damn tough. All I saw was an empty cab.

I pushed the Packard in a straight line, passed the Saint Agnes Hospital and then turned left onto Wharton. I went right at Wharton Square, meandered onto Delancy Street and chugged quietly along a strip of fancy, overpriced restaurants.

Outside somewhere calling itself the Candy Club I got cut off by a big, solid-looking limousine that had a right-hand transmission and RR monogrammed on its radiator grille and hubcaps. I toed the brake and double-parked in front of the

Rolls. I was getting jumpy and both me and my automobile were beginning to wander.

It was after three in the morning when I looked at the time again. If someone was tailing me they were doing great.

On the corner of Fulton and Fifth a yellow light from an all-night drugstore fell invitingly through two large plate-glass windows and silently onto the sidewalk. I pulled up to the curb, parked, walked in and made a quartet of customers on bar stools at the counter. There were two men in blue suits with gray hats pulled hard over their eyes. One was sitting next to a redhead in a wine blouse with short sleeves and a low-cut, crescent front. All three were smoking and drinking black coffee. There were two silver urns, a service door and lots of bright, buttercup yellow paint. The counter was triangular with stools all around. The wall beneath the windows was tiled in the same gastric yellow. It was like being inside a giant cheese.

A ruddy-faced counterman with pronounced bones, thin skin and a bow tie was washing cups in the sink. A tuft of springy-looking, sand-colored hair jutted out from a slim white hat, which stuck to his head at a rakish angle. His ears were big and red and had fair hair sprouting from them. He was in his late thirties and pleased to see me. At three in the morning he was pleased to see anyone.

I ordered coffee and sat a long way from the others. It was very quiet and peaceful with just the urns busily hissing and the dull clunk of china in soapy water. Now and then the man with the woman muttered something short under his breath, but she didn't reply. She played with an empty book of matches, staring hard at it from time to time, like she expected to see something revealing on its cover.

Through the large windows I had a clear view of the street. Some cars drifted lazily by. One of them was a prowl car with two men in uniform. They both looked asleep.

I ordered some more coffee and thought a bit about the briefcase.

Somewhere between the Three Sixes and Maag's Hotel it went missing. The journey takes less than half an hour and the land mass supports one, maybe two million people. Any one of them could have it. Hotel thieves in Camden breed like rats and steal everything they can carry. If Frank Summers had the case when he checked in, he wouldn't have had it long. He was juiced to the gills and my guess was that he would have fallen into a heavy, drunken sleep soon after calling his wife. That way he would have been a sitting duck, child's play and easy meat. And more. But when I found Frank Summers he still had his billfold, his gold fillings and his shoe laces.

It didn't add up.

I put some change on the counter and gave my brain the rest of the night off.

Back in the street I dug around for a cigarette. I was out. There was a dispenser on the wall of the bar and I thumbed a couple of nickels in the slot and pulled out the tray. I was halfway back to my automobile when someone with a gun started firing it at me. He fired three times.

The first slug smacked into the brickwork above my head, leaving a fresh, salmon pink chip. The second followed me to the sidewalk, where I belly-flopped and started to crawl on my knees and elbows as close as I could to the shelter of my car. The third bullet clanged into the metal somewhere on the driver's side. I squirmed over the sidewalk and poked my head around the tire. The bullets had come from the black mouth of an alley on the other side of the street, each shot echoing like an explosion in a mining quarry. On one side of the alley was Luigi's Late-Night Dine and Dance and on the other a pharmacy. The pharmacy window was filled with giant bulbous bottles of translucent red, blue and green liquid, lit as by magic. An illuminated sign read, "Ex-Lax for Relief." Another sign read, "Prescriptions Made Up Here." You notice things like that, lying on the sidewalk at three in the morning, with bullets flying everywhere.

When no more slugs came I got up, ran across the street, and pushed myself hard against the wall of the Dine and Dance. I pulled out my gun, dropped down onto one knee and edged into the gloomy alley. There was no exit that I could see, just piles of garbage cans and a high wooden fence. There was a single light over the service door, which was down a short flight of concrete steps. Everything was suddenly as peaceful and serene as a picnic on a mountainside. But the silence didn't last. A white flame flickered from the service door and coughed another lump of lead noisily into space. The missile screamed close enough to burn my right ear. Instinctively I squeezed the trigger of my own gun and heard a low, human moan. The report died on the air.

I eased along the alley, pressing myself into the shadows, creeping along the wall as if I were walking a ledge a hundred feet above ground. I could feel my heart beating loudly and the air wheezing through my stringy lungs. I moved very carefully, tense, waiting for the black tip of a barrel to point from around the service door and blow me away. But it didn't show. Instead I heard some shouts from inside what I guessed was the kitchen.

I jumped the flight of steps and kicked open the service door, which opened into a long dingy passageway. One side was lined with rows of cardboard boxes of canned food. The tiled walls needed a hosing down, and the smell of stale fat was thicker and heavier than a Californian fog. Two lights burned dimly under frosted glass shades. But it was still very dark. At the end of the passage was a pair of thick wooden doors on two-way hinges with circular windows and steel protective sheets running along the bottom edges.

The doors suddenly burst open to reveal the dark, shadowy shape of a man with a big pistol. He pointed it at me and without hesitating fired his fifth bullet. I threw myself into a gap between a tall pile of cases filled with Joan of Arc kidney beans and some cases of canned fruit. The bullet sang down the passageway and out into the night. The gunman in the doorway was using something big and noisy. A gun like my own: probably a .38, with a slightly longer barrel.

I tore open a case of beans and picked out a can. There was a stencil of Joan of Arc on a horse waving a flag on the side of the packing case. It didn't say a lot for martyrdom. You got roasted to death and ended up as a brand name for the Illinois Canning Co., Hoopston. But I had my own martyrdom to worry about. I counted three shells in my chamber and I assumed he only had a single. I put a solid grip on the can of beans and pitched it hard along the passageway at the doors. I heard it smash into the woodwork as I jumped back between the cases. His last slug boomed into the cans above my head. I sprang into the passage and fired once. But the bullet thumped into empty, swinging doors.

I chased down the narrow corridor, the air reeking with the sharp tang of cordite, and noticed spots of freshly spilled blood on the dirty linoleum floor. My first shot must have been on target.

In the kitchen two fat men were hugging each other like shipwrecked victims on a very small raft. One had on a tall chef's hat and an apron with stripes, and the other was almost changed into the clothes he was going home in.

The chef with the hat said, "Please, mista, donna shoot. A wife. Bambinos. Six, I got." His lips were trembling and the rest of his flabby body was shaking right down to the soles of his roped shoes.

"A man. A man with a rod," I shouted as the Italian dance band on the other side of a second set of swinging doors wound down to a ragged finish. "Which way did he go?"

The chef with the hat pointed a finger at the second set of doors. The other man blinked and grabbed his companion tighter.

"*Mama mia,*" the second man bleated, his face contorted with fear. "Another crazy guy with a gun. Like one is not enough for one night."

A large pan of uncooked french fries had spilled across the floor. Spots of blood stained the slices at regular intervals. The trail led to where the chef had pointed.

I pushed into the dine and dance area. It was a large room with a lot less light than you needed to read the tab clearly. The whole place was decorated to look like a Tuscany farmyard. A couple of rows of tables were placed in a semicircle around the dance floor. The walls were covered with false vines and olive trees and paintings of coy-eyed donkeys pulling little carts loaded with casks of wine. Candles flickered miserably in Chianti bottles, and some onions hung from the low ceiling. That was about it. There were a few people edging toward the hat-check and some others giving their feet a break or finishing their drinks. On the bandstand, half a dozen musicians with embroidered vests and shirts with frilly fronts and gathered sleeves were putting away violins, accordions and double basses into a collection of tattered black cases. The singer was patting his belly and smiling at the departing customers like his next job was something big at the Met.

I didn't see a man with a gun anywhere.

The trail of blood led through Luigi's Dine and Dance and out into the street. It led to the curb and stopped. Someone had driven it away.

It didn't make sense. If I knew where the briefcase was, there was no point in shooting me. So who else could it be? As far as I knew the only enemy I had was the phone company for not paying my bill. But they didn't bump people off, they just wrote letters.

I went back into the club through the front entrance and found the lobby deserted except for the hat-check girl who was putting on a blue wool coat over her peasant blouse and full, floral skirt. A big yellow button with the name Maria was pinned to her blouse.

"Speak English?" I said.

"I'm off," she said, in pure Bronx. "Two minutes ago. No more hats, no more coats. My little world is empty once more. Come back tomorrow."

I took five bucks out of my wallet and laid them on the counter next to a few numbered tickets with a spike through them.

She looked at the money and looked at me with a pair of hard, steady eyes. They were the only part of her body that moved.

"That will buy my left toe," she said. She had dark eyes and dark hair tied up with ribbons. She was older than she looked.

"I've just been shot at," I said. "Out in back. You didn't

hear because your tenor was strangling a lovely old Italian song in a register his voice needed oxygen to reach. The man who shot at me was shadowlike, sort of slim with a gun like mine. A .38 Detective Special. He must have run this way. Maybe he had put his gun away by the time he reached here. He was also wounded—shot in the leg, or in the arm, perhaps. I shot him after he shot at me. Self-defense. The dough is for information. Honest."

She didn't move more than an eyelid.

"Lay off the house wine, chum," she said with a worn-out sigh. "I know it's not my job to tell you, but it rots a guy's brains if he drinks too much." She picked up the five notes and placed them efficiently in a small handbag.

"I'll look after these for a while," she said. Then she put her face close to mine and said, "Now beat it, brother, or there'll be some law here. You can tell them about the guns and the shooting and they will be a lot more interested than me."

With that, she jerked up the flap of the counter, sidled through the gap and flounced out into the street.

I waited until she had flagged down a cab and then took a careful stroll back to my Packard. I examined the driver's door and found a lump of lead buried in the paintwork. I opened the door and hit the spot from inside with the underside of my fist. The flat-nosed missile fell onto the street like a shelled pea. It was a .38. I put it in my pocket and drove home.

21

It was just getting light when I parked.

If someone wanted me dead they could do it while I slept. All my limbs ached mightily and I felt I could faint from fatigue.

My bed was in a rented room over Charlie's Bar. I didn't think I could make the three flights. My office was only two. I reminded myself that Elaine Damone might need me in a hurry. So I settled, not for the first time, for forty winks in the desk chair.

I pulled off my shoes, stuck my heels on the desk and put my chin into my chest. I tipped my hat over my eyes and let myself float into a dream.

I was alone on the stage of La Scala, Milan. The vast auditorium was dark and empty. There were a few props, wooden boxes and some sacks. I was dressed in a costume of a character from Beethoven's *Fidelio*. I was Floristan, the hero, lying on the sacks with a ball and chain around my ankle. From the orchestra pit the sound of a tango band began playing a slow, erotic dance tune, the violin wailing with an almost human sound. As the stilted tango rhythm cranked on, naked female dancers melted out of the misty gloom. In the center of the troupe stood Elaine Damone. She was Leonora in a slinky silver cocktail dress with a long sexy slit up one side. As the stage lights brightened, I could see she was holding a large cigarette box. The lights turned from red to a cold blue to a sickly yellow and the dancers moved their supple bodies in awkward patterns, angular and grotesque. Suddenly Elaine pointed a finger at me. The dancers, as one body, turned and began crawling and slithering toward me. I tried to call out, to sing, but no words came. The dancers grew nearer and I saw that their faces were those of demented dogs with blood-stained teeth and horrible, swollen eyes. I kicked furiously with my legs, trying to move as the demonic creatures were almost upon me.

Then from the wings a trumpet sounded, sweet and clear. The dancers instantly vanished as Beethoven's villain, Pizarro, strutted on in a harlequin's mask and began embracing Elaine Damone with disgusting, carnal urgency. She was laughing, wildly, as she let her long leg slip through the slit in her dress, hooking it around the back of Pizarro's thighs. The house lights went up and revealed a packed house of convicts in striped fatigues. They were standing and shouting and banging tin dinner plates with pool balls. Pizarro was singing like Gobbi. Melodies flowed as easily and effortlessly as the Missouri River. As I tried to escape, the ball and chain grew bigger and heavier with each movement.

Then the spotlight fell on me. The crowd immediately stopped applauding. First it went quiet, then it went dark once more, and then the air was filled with pool balls, which rained down and smashed into my helpless body.

Then a fight referee in a dicky and black tie was peering over me and saying the bell had saved me. Indeed, the sound of a bell was almost deafening.

My phone was ringing more urgently than a fire alarm.

I opened a bleary eye and let my bleary gaze fall on the wrist that told the time. It said half-past seven. My head was throbbing and my mouth felt like I had been chewing mustard seeds. I couldn't speak. I picked up the phone, all of it, and dropped it into the desk drawer. It didn't stop ringing; it just rang quieter. I didn't like the noise. It was the kind of ring that didn't have a voice I wanted to talk to on the other end. So I didn't answer it.

Instead I went to the john down the hall, where I splashed myself with water, dried my hands with a sheet of tissue, washed my mouth by letting water from the faucet pour straight in and gave myself a once-over in the mirror, which was balanced on two rusty nails over the basin. The face that stared back looked almost human. Some of it would only scare small dogs, and a cosmetic surgeon would maybe think twice before taking a buck off me. With a few hours sleep in the bank I was beginning to feel like a fight. I stuck a cigarette between my lips, lit it, sucked hard and went back to my desk.

The phone was still ringing. It shocked me a little. I opened the drawer and took the instrument out. Then I placed it on the desk and picked up the receiver.

It was a woman's voice, but not Elaine's. Nor the hot little blonde from Ardmore. It was an operator. She said, "Is this Mike Dime? I have a call for you."

I said it was and the line went dead for a second. Then there were some clicks that didn't interest me, and my mind began to wander to thoughts of breakfast and a shave.

The second voice that spoke wasn't really a voice at all. Not in the strict sense of the word. The sound seemed to bypass the larynx and emerge from a gap somewhere in the side of the throat. The noise was like air from a punctured tire or gas from a leaking pipe. The voice was a wheezy, disgusting gasp. It seemed to crawl down the wire and wind itself round my neck and tighten, like a hungry boa constrictor. But whatever made words said, "We have some important business to discuss, Mr. Dime. Very important business. Write down this address and pay me a visit. Do it now. Not later on, when you fancy, but now."

I scribbled some names and numbers on the scratch pad and said that I had done so. There was a short pause.

"Good," the throat gasped, seemingly with a great deal of effort. "Do nothing silly, like telling the cops or leaving messages under stones. That will just make me angry. Don't get smart. Just get over here. And tell me what I want to know."

The line went dead. I hung up. There was no need for me to add anything.

With Warren Ratenner there never would be.

It was a run-down block with a demolition order on it about two miles in from where the Delaware bends east, upriver, past Mud Island and Delanco on the New Jersey side, past the yacht clubs of Wissinoming, Quaker, Riverton, Forest Hill, Columbia and Dredge Harbor.

A lot of bricks were already mountains of rubble and the air was thick with dust. Three sides of one tall building were torn away, exposing rising layers of interior walls that looked strangely naked, almost embarrassed without the protection of a front door and ceiling and a nice old lady to say, come in and wipe your feet first.

There weren't a lot of people around and the handful of souls that I saw looked aimless. Most of them were black. It was still too early for workmen to be on the site. Two brightly painted orange bulldozers sat motionless at careless angles on heaps of debris. And in the middle of the rubble a giant crane with a massive ball dangling from a chain attached to the tip of the arm stood proudly, like a twentieth century totem pole. It looked like the kind of toy a kid would want to operate when he grew up. It would be more fun than driving a fire engine.

It was all very still and silent and calm, like a room after a death.

I parked at a gas station that was part of the demolition site. There were no pumps or fixtures, just a few split tires and some other oily garbage. It was attached to what was once a wreckers' yard that was stripped of anything worth stripping.

I got out of the car and walked through the empty garage

into the yard. The place looked like it had not been in use for a long time. There were wide cracks in the concrete filled with clumps of yellow-tipped weeds. It was about the size of a football field and strewn with abandoned, heavily rusting prewar automobiles. They looked like the bones of slain buffalo. A 1933 Pierce-Arrow was trying to hang onto its pedigree with a thinning coat of silver paint that was only just beating off rust. It was probably doing a better job of looking elegant than the rich dames who got driven around in it. There was a Nash sedan with its busted grille looking like a set of rotten teeth and a 1936 Chevrolet picked clean of every last accessory, from the ashtrays to the vanity mirror.

You would see sights like that forever.

Beyond the wreckers' yard was a maze of small huts and wooden sheds. There were some brick buildings that had been built more recently. But they were vacant and every single window had a set of black, jagged holes. I was looking for a warehouse with a sign saying Canton Imports.

A light wind was blowing a cold drizzle in from the north and a weak sun was trying to get noticed between two fists of solid cloud. I pulled up my collar and pushed on through the low huts, to see the warehouse I wanted a hundred yards to my right.

It had only one entrance not covered by wood slats or corrugated iron sheets. It was at the side of the building at the foot of an iron fire escape. My gun was under my arm but it was still empty from the night before. It didn't worry me. I had been tailed from the second I left Tasker Street and there were eyes watching me now. It was quiet, but the kind of quiet of men standing very still, not of emptiness.

Anyway, I had come for a chat, to talk over a few things. Who would need a gun? There was going to be no unpleasantness. We were grown-up men. Guns were for the boys. I went on like that for a little while but I didn't convince myself.

I pushed open a metal door with rusty rivets and stepped into the landing at the foot of a steep staircase. It was suddenly dark, but I could see a door leading into the lower storeroom to my left. A powerful smell of mixed spices filled the air. Cumin and coriander, saffron, cinnamon, fragrances that suggested Eastern bazaars, cool Arabian interiors full of silk cushions and dusky, sultry women in tissue-thin gowns.

Something hard and familiar poked me between my shoulder blades.

"Wake up, bud," a voice said. "Mr. Ratenner is waiting. Keep your noise pointing straight ahead and no one will get hurt."

It wasn't Sinbad the Sailor.

"Don't you want me to throw my gun on the floor?" I said without moving. "Throw it real slow and easy, you know the way?"

"You don't have to worry about that," the voice behind me said. "You ain't gonna have no time to mess around with any guns. That's my job. Let me tell you the gun I got is all sawed-off at one end and the trigger is sorta old and loose. Real wobbly. Least little twitch and off she goes. Boom! one barrel. Boom! barrel number two. Blows holes the size of cow pats. Blow you into next year. No, bud. You leave your gun where it is and climb the stairs to the top floor."

I started to climb the stone steps between dirty brown brick walls, whitewashed from the floor up to the handrail. I counted six floors to the top and the smell of spice grew fainter with each landing.

"Been in Philly long?" I said halfway up. "Chicago has become such a dull place with Big Al gone and Mayor Kennelly being such a wet fish and all. Never mind. They'll elect Daley in a year or so and the joint will start jumping again."

"You talk too much," the voice from the Windy City said. "I told Mr. Ratenner I was all for blowin' your brains out right from the start."

"Too bad," I said. "I should write to your congressman about it. Better still, get real mad and blow Mr. Ratenner's brains out. That way I can get on with my nothing life in peace and you can spend the rest of the day doing whatever takes your fancy. There's a new Bob Hope movie downtown at the Plaza, and the Eagles are hanging around Veterans Stadium looking for someone to beat. You could get a few of your boys together and pick up some appearance money."

"I sure wish Mr. Ratenner would let me blow your brains out."

I didn't say anything more after that.

We stopped in front of another metal door like the one at the bottom of the stairs. The room on the other side had probably been a cold storage. It was half open, and no light came from the Stygian darkness in the gap between the door and its iron frame.

"In you go, bud," the gunman said encouragingly. "Not too slow and not too fast."

"Nice and easy," I said.

"That's the way."

I pulled open the door and the butt of the gun behind me kicked me hard in the small of my back. I stumbled in the ghostly, lightless space and fell to the floor, put my hand out and grabbed a lump of wood. It was attached to other bits of wood. It was a chair. I couldn't see it, but it felt that way.

There was a long silence and then Ratenner spoke. He spoke as he had on the phone, his words formed as if squeezed from some venomous source.

"Give Mr. Dime a seat, boys, and don't kill him till I say kill him."

There were other men in the room but they had been there long enough for their eyes to grow used to the impenetrable gloom. One man grabbed a handful of my hair and pulled me up while another hit me in the stomach. I bent double and almost threw up. I sagged a little and felt the seat of the chair thrust against my calves. The hand in my hair held tight, and as a naked bulb burst into life it jerked my head so that my eyes saw nothing but the bright glare. The only way to avoid being blinded was by closing my eyes, which seemed to be what Warren Ratenner wanted.

"Smart," he breathed. "I see you. You don't see me." He laughed. It sounded like he had a throat full of snakes.

"Now hear me good, Dime," Ratenner hissed. "I hate words. They cost me effort. They take up time. So I only say a thing once."

There was the rustle of paper, crinkly paper, like cellophane. Then Warren Ratenner said, "A couple of nights back I get a call from one of my boys who tells me he has had some trouble with a very important package of mine. He is phoning from an apartment of a dame whose old man has somehow got mixed up in my business transactions. My boy tells me that a private dick called Dime is also mixed up in it and that he is expected to shed a little light on why a certain bag of mine has vanished. That's what he says. He also says he will be bringing the dick along to answer a few questions with relation to the aforementioned bag. But my boys don't show. I don't hear another word until I pick up today's rag in the barber shop and see a picture of my boys being wheeled into a meat wagon. So I give you a call."

"Neat," I said.

In the darkness outside my closed eyes I heard the sound of jaws exercising themselves, loudly, like they were eating something wet. Then there was the rich smell of cigar smoke, heavy and full of nice things. Ratenner had been sucking the end, making sure that the leaves didn't flake off. It was a regular cigar smoker's trick.

"We don't have a lot of time," Ratenner said over a long puff of smoke. "And you have the least of anyone I know."

"I don't have your briefcase either," I said. "I assume that is what this barn dance is all about—the reason I am sitting here with a goon yanking my hair out by the roots."

Ratenner said, "You are here because I told you to come, Dime. No other reason."

There was a short silence which wasn't so quiet that I couldn't hear the man thinking. His thoughts were deep, and whatever he thought, he did. The two were one in Warren Ratenner.

"Like I told you," he went on, sucking on his cigar—sucking on his words, too. "Your time is almost through. But I will offer you a reprieve. All you got to do is bring my briefcase here exactly twenty-four hours from now. If you don't it's down the pan with the reprieve, and my boys will start the work for which they are famous."

He laughed again, a kind of echolike laugh that ended with his lungs fighting for air.

"That's all," he said at last, his words thick with sputum. "I don't care if you have the briefcase or don't have the briefcase. It's all the same to me. Just bring it."

"Gift-wrapped or brown paper bag?"

"You disappoint me, Dime. Really disappoint me."

"I disappoint a lot of people," I said. "Have since I was knee high to a ground-nut. High school, confirmation classes, police department, Ike's army. A big disappointment, right down the line. I'm the biggest disappointment this side of Little Big Horn."

"You're a dead man, Dime."

"You got the wrong stooge, Ratenner," I said. "Every bit wrong. Besides, I already got a job and my employer has got more charm than you and your boys all rolled into one. She pays a hundred a day for my trouble and what's more she talks about painting and plays the piano. She probably tucks a cordon bleu under her apron and does a lot of other things a single guy like me would be interested in. Find someone else to dig up Philly and shake down all the big- and small-time hoods. I'm booked up with some class."

A wall of smoke, heavy with Ratenner's foul breath, hit me in the face. I coughed a little.

"You're a real cute egg," Ratenner said. "You think you are really something. A big heart in gumshoes. All fancy talk and dames tripping over themselves to rent your charm. Well, let me tell you something. I've got an operation that's razor sharp and it works smooth because I keep it simple and I keep it to myself. It works because I know what makes a sucker bite and just how much he can chew before choking. I know a lot more. Everyone loves something. With some people it's stamps. With others it's a dog or a rose bush. Some people care for things and don't know it, that is until it ain't there no more. That's most people, Dime. People like you.

Your tough act don't fool me no more than a magician in a top hat sawing through a box with a doll hanging out each end. You can kid yourself with your hammy lines and you might be dumb enough to believe them. But I know different."

He let out a chuckle, controlled, so as not to start his lungs from spilling over again.

"You are a dog, Dime," he went on. "A dog who knows he is on his last scraggy legs but won't lay down. A dog who sticks his damp nose in the first hand that throws him a bone. I've asked around, Dime. They tell me that without a pat on the head from time to time you would have drunk yourself under a headstone the day they hung a Purple Heart around your neck and kicked you back home. Make no mistake. I'll find who is pulling your leash. It will take no time at all."

I was going to say something but when I opened my mouth there was nothing coming out. The hook was in and Ratenner knew it. Some faces of people I knew flashed across my mind. Then Frank Summers's face appeared. And then a bit more of him. He was holding a banner. It said: REMEMBER WHAT RATENNER DID TO NORMA AND ME. Thanks, Frank, how could I forget? But I am in a frame. Ratenner wants something I don't have. The same thing he wanted from you. Maybe you got some bright ideas, like who might have his briefcase of loot now. Give the matter some thought, buddy. Run it up the flagpole and when you have something I can use, pop around and see me. You know where I am. Only don't leave it too long. Not later than the day after tomorrow.

I could hear the scrape of a chair as someone stood up quickly. Even with my eyelids shut tight, the glare from the bulb created a fire red haze. The heat it generated was surprising. No hotter than Death Valley in June.

Then Ratenner said, "Don't spend too much time thinking about it, Dime. Do it. It's A-B-C simple. Bring my briefcase and every last one of its contents to this exact same room precisely twenty-four hours from now. Fail and you can kiss someone close good-bye. You have cost me two good boys. More important, you have wasted a lot of my very precious time. But precious though it is there is still a little left. You, Dime, have just . . . eighty-seven thousand seconds. So long, smart boy. Start counting."

As Ratenner finished speaking, a lump of something hard and soulless thumped my skull. A high whine sounded for a brief second. I opened my eyes to the white, explosive light, like a photographer's flash had been fired full in my face. Then my eyes fell out and rolled into a dark corner. Me and my consciousness had gone our separate ways.

I woke up shivering to an empty room, the light still burning brightly from a single bulb, hanging like an illuminated spider. There was a table, two chairs and half a Havana cigar. That was all. There was me, of course, although I didn't know that for sure. All I knew about myself was the gap in the back of my head where the blood had gone out and the pain had come in. But it had to be me hopelessly trying to stand erect, like Pleistocene man illustrating Darwin's theory of the origin of species. No one else I knew would be so dumb.

At last I got upright and dusted myself off. Then for no reason I could think of at the time, I decided to drop me and my split head on Elaine Damone.

On the way I thought of some reasons. And they were pretty damn cute at that.

23

A foot-high marble figurine was dancing on Elaine Damone's mantelpiece, her light pink body balancing effortlessly on one dainty toe. Her left leg was bent at the knee and raised high, like a drum majorette marching. Her limbs were elongated, extra smooth and stylized as in African sculpture. Her face was high-cheeked and full-lipped, obviously Negroid. But the hair was long, carved in neat wavy rows and swept back from the forehead as if blown by a strong wind. The elegant line of the coiffure was echoed in the base, a thick-ribbed, veined marble scallop. Above her head the figurine was holding a black marble disc rimmed in gold with twelve thin gold strips radiating from its center at regular intervals. Two more strips of gold were moving imperceptibly. They told the time. They said it was just after ten.

A Chinese maid with skin the color of peanut butter and a cherry blossom pink pair of lips told me to wait while she informed Miss Damone that there was a visitor who was not expected. She had shown me into the living room with a face that the Chinese are famous for and brushed off my early morning smile like it was an ant on her foot.

I was halfway through a cigarette when the maid returned.

"Miss Damone taking bath," she said. "But will see you first."

She was built small and carried a lot of very white, petal-shaped teeth outside her mouth. Behind her stood Elaine Damone.

"Run along, Lilly," she said to the Oriental. "And put out another towel. I imagine Mr. Dime could use something wet for his head."

Lilly vanished without a word.

"I could use something wet for my mouth," I said tentatively, patting the wound and feeling the lumps of caked blood in my hair.

She walked to the place where she kept liquor.

She was wearing a kingfisher blue wrap-around negligee in pure silk. The vee-neck bodice was pleated and cut very low, front and back, and belted behind. The long, open line gave Elaine Damone's tanned cleavage a lot of air. Her hair was uncombed and looked wild and uncontrollable. Her eyes, large and clear, were not made up and were dark as a moonless night.

"You have clearly ignored my instructions," Elaine Damone said sharply. "My brother's blackmail is a very serious business and you are the one person between us—that is, the Damone family—and complete disaster. Is it really too much to ask that you keep out of trouble for more than five minutes at a time?"

"It's a long story," I said. "And it has nothing to do with blackmailers or your family or your family's good name or the fact that your brother is a rotten apple."

"I am very pleased to hear it," she said, mixing a lot of pale liquid with orange juice, ice and a pile of chopped fruit.

"By the way," she added. "Don't think for a second I wish to be inhospitable, but what brings you to my home at this ungodly hour? You haven't said."

So I told her. But not so that it would worry her that early in the day. I said that I was working simultaneously on a job that involved finding a briefcase some guy had lost and that he and I had seen things differently for a while, the way guys do, and we sort of didn't shake hands to resolve our differences, and instead he sort of slugged me. It was a sort of gentlemen's agreement. A token gesture of goodwill in place of a down payment. I rambled on like that for a bit and she listened with more attention than I really deserved. She filled me up from time to time, big shots of the pale stuff, and sat in her seat under the window. She nodded here and there to let me know that she was concerned. But beautiful women with breeding always listen politely when men run off at the mouth. If it's been a bore they say so at the end, not in the middle. But Elaine wasn't finding it hard work, dull as it seemed to me. She was all ears.

When I had finished talking she got up and came close to me. Her body was warm and I could smell her skin, lightly scented with musk. But it wasn't from a bottle.

"Lilly is running a bath. I suggest you use it to clean up the wound. And you might like to take the opportunity of washing the rest of you while you're there. The kind of private investigators I employ should not smell quite so . . . masculine. By the way, I have still heard nothing from the blackmailer creature. You don't suspect anything has gone wrong, do you?"

I said, "These people take their time. They play games. Making you sweat is part of the psychological game. They like you to roast for a while. That way you panic more and think less. Once you start thinking, there is a chance you might get smart and do something clever. Something to ruin their fun. I suggest you stay as cool as you are and my bet is that he'll call soon enough."

She seemed only half convinced but she let it go at that.

"Lilly will show you where the tub is," she said. "Take your drink along. I'll be in my bedroom. I have some things to do, letters to write and so forth. Take your time bathing. If you want anything, Lilly will be at hand."

Elaine Damone gave me a smile and left the room.

Lilly was in the alcove.

"Step this way," she said. "Bathwater velly hot."

The bathroom was the inspiration of a demented Aztec with a hangover. It was a large, hollow, octagonal room with the floor filled by a circular, sunken tub big enough to keep a school of whales happy. It was a plush affair smothered in tiny turquoise and gold mosaic. There were animals on the bottom, mainly pink frogs with square, angular legs and silver snakes with their cold eyes picked out in pyrite. In the center of the design was a giant golden sun with its rays the shape of snipped-off spear heads. The windowless room was full of moody intimacy, the way women like it when they bathe. Quiet and solitary. A place to be completely alone, to do just what they want. It felt good sharing that. The artificial light was so dusky and discreet I couldn't see where the diffused lamps were hidden. A little light came from just under the rim of the tub. An emerald glass fillet was set into the wall an inch or two above the overflow. Behind the glass were powerful spotlights that turned the steamy surface of the water the color of crème de menthe. The walls of the room were faced with smooth black slabs of polished marble, edged with custard yellow and vermilion glazed tiles top and bottom. The panels were inlaid with fine gold outlines of half-naked male deities in awkward, semi-sitting, semi-leaping postures. Their heads were a mixture of feathers and vast plumes and tropical flowers. They held highly decorative javelins and other weapons. But they weren't killing anyone with them, just having a party.

The faucet was concealed under a huge imitation human skull, encrusted with bands of turquoise and jet. The eye sockets were gold and silver. You pressed the gold and hot water poured from the open mouth. Cold came from pressing the silver.

"Thank you, Lilly," I said. "I'll get the hang of it."

She vanished again and I undressed.

There were no mirrors except for the ceiling, which was all mirror. Dark peach tint engraved with frosted moons and fabulous birds. The green water rippled in the reflection and a sweet smell of lime and jasmine hung faintly in the misty, heated air.

I slithered into the water and let my nerve ends have a good swig, like desert flowers in the rain. The warmth felt like an all-over caress, or like the sun on the first day of summer.

For the first time in three days I didn't feel like a composer writing counterpoint going in opposite directions—Ratenner and his mob one way and Elaine Damone's family the other. Ratenner had played his opening hand and it was a lot of aces. And there were a few more up his sleeve, hidden in his vest, tucked behind his ear. Ratenner had aces like church steeples have death-watch beetles. But Harvey Hendersson's theory on Manny Gluck's operation suggested that the man at the top had a man in the middle to deal with the man at the bottom. And to get pedantic, I hadn't actually seen Ratenner. I had spoken to someone calling himself Ratenner on the phone and later had met him. But my eyes were shut. He could have been anyone, for all I knew. Anyone from Harpo Marx to Artie Shaw.

But if my brain was struggling, my muscles were doing great. They were humming sweeter than a barbershop quartet as the hot water rolled down the lumps and smoothed away the ache. I was on the very edge of falling into a deep slumber that would have had Rip Van Winkle looking for another job when, with a jolt, I realized something else didn't fit.

Ratenner's boys could not have been responsible for the shooting incident outside Luigi's Dine and Dance. That was a definite attempt at assassination: the bullets were much too close to be taken as a warning broadside. And a warning of what? Ratenner clearly wanted me alive, at least for the time being. Alive, he thought I could help him. Dead, I'd just help undertakers.

The conclusion I reached was that either the shadowy man with the gun and the wound was settling some score I didn't know about, or it was a bad case of mistaken identity. It was possible. After all, I'd been wearing a clean suit and a new shirt.

The water in the tub had begun to cool a little so I pushed a big toe into the gold eye on the skull. Hot water gushed out in a noisy, solid jet and filled the room with steam, making it as dense as a Highland mist. I unfolded and almost floated on my back in the bright green water. I was just beginning to wish I had a goldfish or some Mickey Mouse soap to play with when I realized that I wasn't alone. Through the mist I saw a shape with curves on each side. It was a shape around 36-24-36 and stood around five-eight. It was probably twenty-eight or twenty-nine years old and had a slight soft lisp when it spoke. It said in a voice that was as matter-of-fact as a stenographer reading back her notes, "Did you ever learn Archimedes' principle? He discovered that the weight of a submerged body displaced an equal weight of water. He was in his tub at the time that he made his discovery. He was so thrilled that he ran out into the street and told everyone, just as he was. Now what do you think of that?"

She didn't wait for an answer and I didn't have one anyway.

"Move over," Elaine Damone said, and the amount of water displaced by the weight of the submerged bodies in the tub was suddenly doubled.

"I don't want you to run away with the idea that your client is one of those girls," she said through the thick wall of steam.

"What kind of a girl is one of those girls?" I said hopelessly.

A hand of wide, spread-open fingers pressed hard against my stomach and began to massage it in confident, circular movements.

"This kind of girl," she said. When she spoke the word *this*, it came out *thith*, somehow evoking the memory of a long lost childhood, of lost, faded dreams. It was a world that began and ended in innocent young girls with soft, golden curls and prim summer frocks in forget-me-not blue; tanned, bare legs covered in the finest, palest yellow down. That was all they wore. But were there so many, or just one alone? Or not even one?

Whatever the answer, there was nothing innocent about Elaine Damone. Absolutely nothing.

24

I was sitting in a chair made from two bits of red and blue plywood stuck in a black wooden frame, the edges of which had been dipped in a bright dandelion yellow. It felt more comfortable than it looked. A lot of tasteful tinted glass and thin strips of lead put together by Tiffany sat on a square occasional table at my elbow. The lamp was not switched on as there was still plenty of daylight remaining. Almost a complete afternoon of it. I was smoking and holding a book by Ernest Hemingway, open at the first page. I had read the first couple of paragraphs about thirty or forty times, but nothing had registered. I think they were about a bullfighter finding the secret of life in the sweat, the sand and the blood of the bullring. The book had an unusual bookmark, a glossy print of two people, a man and a woman, doing nothing in particular. They looked like the kind of people Hemingway would have had a lot in common with. The man looked tough and the woman looked beautiful.

Elaine Damone was still in her bedroom getting dressed. And she was taking her time. Nothing in that. All women care about their clothes, and most of them care about how they put them on. Some dress for their sweethearts, their husbands, their lovers. Some dress for other women. Some dress for themselves. Elaine Damone dressed like she was about to be inspected by a platoon of GIs, ten Hollywood producers, Mr. Universe, the gang at Lindy's, the head waiter at the Georges Cinq, the Duke and Duchess of Windsor and an eighteen-year-old motor mechanic eating his lunch. None of them would find a speck out of place.

When Elaine walked into sight she was wearing a navy blue blouse with pin-head lemon yellow dots. The front was cut low and buttoned three times. It was tucked into a pair of high-waisted, salmon pink slacks. There was a string of pearls as long as a tow rope wound around her neck, and two pearls, the same two I had seen the night she picked me up, were attached to the soft rounded lobes of her ears. Her hair was still wet and she had combed it straight back off her forehead and tied it in a long, loose pony tail. There was an emerald ring that I had not seen before on the middle finger of her left hand and an emerald and pearl bracelet around the wrist of her right arm. Both pieces of jewelry were antique and not the least bit showy. A go-when-you-like look was just peeping through her hospitality. So far she was keeping it under control.

"There is some breakfast," she said coldly. "If it's not too late to call it that. Eggs, coffee, orange juice."

"Something to give me back my strength," I said, and stubbed my cigarette into a large, sea green glass dish.

I snapped Hemingway shut. It made the sound of someone pounding a pillow. "Before I get fatted up I need to use a phone. There is a guy I know with tin legs and more heart than a stage of vaudeville troupers who is hoping to get some information that may help me. He plays pool, and between hobbling around the tables and pocketing everything in sight, he keeps his ears open. Most of the scum and hoodlums in this town pass through his arena so there is an outside chance he may even be able to give me something for you."

"That would be nice," she said without much interest. Like she was making a dinner date with someone she didn't know too well. Or like much. "Join me in the kitchen when you have made your call. You know where it is."

She turned and left me alone to phone Joey Pozo.

There was a long gap between my dialing and Max picking up the phone at the other end. Only it wasn't Max.

"Hold the line," the voice said before I spoke. "Who is calling?"

I said my name and waited some more. Finally Max Slovan came to the phone.

"Mike," he said huskily. "Been some trouble. Been calling you all morning. Get down here fast as you can. The cops are filling the joint with blue. They wanna talk to you." He hung up.

He didn't have to tell me there had been trouble. Bad news has a way of being aired that doesn't need words.

I put the receiver into the cradle, very gently, very slowly, like it would explode if banged too hard. My hands had gone clammy and my heart was pounding fast, as if I had just run up a lot of stairs. I didn't move from the spot. I just stood staring at the phone, seeing nothing but a blank, empty void.

I must have been there a long time. Elaine Damone had come back and was calling to me something about the coffee getting cold, but the sound of her voice hardly registered. Like radio waves during an electric storm.

The muscles in my neck and down my spine were beginning to tighten and become stiff.

"Something the matter?" she asked with just enough concern to show the question was not perfunctory.

I nodded and tried to smile. But it didn't work out as a smile. More of weak grimace, the kind of look kids give when they wet their pants. It was a smile that wouldn't have sold much but helplessness. And I sold that to Elaine Damone.

"I am sorry," she said. "But I must make one thing quite clear. Whatever has happened as a result of your telephone conversation, you have a commitment to me that I have paid for. I must warn you, I shall take firm action if you endanger my confidences or fail to carry out your part in the agreement we have struck. I am aware that there is nothing on paper, but negligence on your behalf would be taken very seriously by those who have authorized your license to operate as a private investigator. If you are not going to be contactable, kindly call me at regular intervals. I do not wish to have my maid involved in any way, and so I will be here to take the message personally."

I heard it all and nodded again.

"I'll call," I said wearily. "The Dime Detective Agency never sleeps. Sometimes it misses out and gets its clients killed, but only sometimes. But I got the feeling this time we're going to hit lucky. A hunch, you might say. What you women call intuition."

"We women know what a hunch is," she said frostily. It was like we had just met. "Just make sure you phone," she added.

I walked with empty legs through Elaine Damone's luxurious apartment, through the long corridor with carpet up to your knees leading to the kitchen. There was the big smell of eggs frying in butter. I was going to miss them. I was going to miss a lot of things. But none as much as the silver picture frame without a picture that used to live on Elaine Damone's mantelpiece.

25

I didn't like the look of what was going on outside Max Slovan's. But somehow I knew it would be like that. There were two prowl cars parked carelessly on each side of the street and an ambulance double-parked. A man in a bright white coat was closing its doors. Some other men with cases and photographers' equipment were hurrying into an official sedan that had its engine running. There were people milling around in small groups, following each stage of the ritual of police work with jerking heads and low mutterings. A slim cop with an overbite and big hands was keeping them in check. When the police car pulled away I caught a glimpse of the coroner for the precinct, a man named Prosser.

There seemed to be cars everywhere and I had to drive almost to the end of the block before I found a parking space. I messed up the reverse, grinding the gears and cracking the brake light shield on the bumper of someone's new mustard-colored Mercury.

It took five minutes to get back to where the cop at the door of Max Slovan's was standing with his hands on his hips, looking up and down the street. The small crowd had grown smaller. It was more or less all over, whatever it was.

I drew level with the cop and made as if to step down into the poolroom.

He put up a palm facing me, like an Indian chief greeting someone. "Joint's shut, bud," he said, looking over my shoulder at no one in particular. His Adam's apple wobbled in a long, thin neck.

"I'm expected," I said. I didn't take it any further, just pushed by and into the room beyond.

"Hey," he shouted after me. "Get your butt outa,there."

"Quit yelling," Max Slovan said. He was standing by the pool table nearest the door, folding up a large gray dust sheet. "This is the guy your boss has been asking for."

His face was very pale and he looked older than I had ever seen him.

The cop gave us both a long, suspicious look. He took off his cap and smoothed down a well-trimmed head of light brown hair. Then he put his cap on with both hands and squinted.

"If you say so," he said, running the tip of his tongue across his teeth. "Only I got my orders."

I said nothing to Max, not a word.

The air was musty and I coughed and heard it echo. I plodded between the rows of silent tables, somber as tombstones. There was a man standing beside the only table with a light burning above it. The table was Joey Pozo's.

There were only three men in the room, four including the outline of a man drawn in white chalk on the bed of Joey Pozo's table. It looked odd, half-finished without legs. The right arm had been either on or under the body, because the chalk line stopped at the elbow. The other arm was at a ninety-degree angle to the shoulder. Its crudely sketched hand had an outstretched finger pointing to the top end of the table where two broken lines of pool balls sat almost hidden under the rubber cushion. There was a thick patch of dried blood in the middle of the green baize. It was the color of rotten plums.

The man by the table introduced himself as Captain Uglo. He'd been recently transferred from somewhere or another and wanted to ask me a few questions, a matter of routine. Something like that. I only heard the odd word. The part of my brain that received information had shut down. Like an ants' nest after it had been violated.

Uglo was a rotund little guy with a bald pate, red cheeks and a thick, badly trimmed mustache that looked glued on—

and at the wrong angle at that. What was left of his hair was darker than you would have expected for a man who was clearly over fifty. It was almost black. He had small, full lips, like a trumpet player, and small, fat fingers, like a pianist. His suit was three-piece and should have been in a museum. The jacket was buttoned over his paunch with the lower button, and the material had to stretch to make it. His jacket pockets bulged like saddlebags. I figured that if he had just been transferred he probably had his desk and filing cabinets and all that stuff in them.

I moved from the table, like someone who had just vomited over the side of a ship, and sank into a chair. Automatically I dug around for a cigarette, found one somewhere and put it on a small table beside my chair.

Uglo took a chair from another table and dragged it over. He reversed it between me and the pool table and straddled it, his short arms dangling over the backrest.

"Buddy of yours?" he said in a low baritone and jerked his head back at the pool table. It was a pleasant voice, one a lot of people would have talked to freely. They would have confessed all sorts of things to it, from rape to arson, from homicide to stealing candy.

"I met him in France," I said, picking up the cigarette and tapping the end on my thumbnail. "Normandy. He was a kid in my squad. We were Rangers. He was a T-5."

Uglo nodded and took a cheroot out of one of his jacket pockets. He looked at it for a second, then rolled it across his bottom lip. "T-5," he said. "Radio op."

Uglo continued rolling his cheroot and I kept tapping my cigarette.

Then he said, "Max Slovan says you dropped in a night back for the first time in an age. He doesn't say, but I say it's mighty peculiar. Twenty-four hours after the old reunion party your buddy eats a slug."

Our eyes met and locked, like antlers on the heads of two cagey stags.

"Got a match?" the captain said, and leaned over the seat.

I fumbled around and came up with my lighter. I handed it to him and he lit his cheroot slowly, never taking his eyes off me for a second. When the tip glowed, Uglo let out a lungful of sweet smelling smoke, directing it sideways from the corner of his mouth.

"Twenty-five cents' worth of heaven," he said. "You can keep your thigh-rolled Havanas. The wops make these. My brother-in-law imports them. Lord knows what they make them with, but they taste a lot better'n they look."

He left the cheroot burning merrily in his mouth and slid both his hands into his jacket pockets. He fumbled and fussed for a while and finally his left hand pulled out a paper bag with the words *Police Dept*. printed in small type across its middle. He held it out at arm's length and emptied the contents onto the small table.

"The deceased's effects," he said. "Not much to go on. No clues as would tell us much about the person or persons who shot him. Or why he was shot."

He pushed the things around with a disappointed finger like someone sorting out the pieces of a jigsaw puzzle. There was a billfold with a few dollars and a V.A. card. There were some cubes of chalk, a few loose coins, some keys and an IOU for thirty bucks. I couldn't read the name.

There was nothing for me.

"What killed him?" I said, still tapping the cigarette.

"A slug from a big bore. Thirty-eight, at a guess."

Uglo began to put the things back into the paper bag, picking them up one at a time.

"What time?"

"Midnight, or thereabouts. They shot him and threw him to die on the table. Nice people you got in Philly." He let some smoke out of his nostrils.

"Nice people everywhere," I said. "Any different where you come from?"

"Oklahoma City," he said. "You seen the musical, you should know. They grow corn and cows. A few people get shot. Most die of boredom."

He put the bag back in his pocket and puffed hard on

the cheroot. It put an extra inch of ash on the end, but it didn't fall off. It was one of those smokes with ash that stays put right to the stump and then lets go with a vengeance, like an avalanche. From the look of the ash stains on Uglo's jacket that happened maybe ten or twenty times a day.

"What brings you to this museum of a town?" I said without a lot of interest. I was looking at the line of balls under the green baize cushion. His eyes caught the direction of my stare and turned his head with some effort, the way fat men do.

"Thought that was curious myself," he said. "Hustlers and pool room pros like my buddy usually stick them back in the triangle or put them in the pockets." He spoke without looking at me. Then he turned and said, "I got a transfer because they got short-staffed somewhere else. There was a choice of a couple of places. I came here because I thought the experience might be useful. Thought I might meet a few hard-boiled private dicks and get on a real juicy homicide. I figured if I could bag a few killers in a hot town like Philly they might elect me commissioner when I got back."

"You'll never make it," I said, "unless you change your tailor. You do have tailors in Oklahoma City?"

"Tailors like this town has hospitals. You must have a lot of sick people."

"Sick in body, sick in mind," I said, without really knowing why.

I finally decided to light the cigarette in my hand but I couldn't find my lighter. Then I remembered I gave it to Uglo.

"You have my lighter," I said and held out my hand.

"Bad habit," he said, taking it from his vest pocket and throwing it the short distance between our chairs. "Had it since I was a kid."

"Pity you're not going to be here longer," I said, lighting up. "I know a couple of boys with leather couches and goatee beards in some of those hospitals you mentioned who would like to hear about it."

I let out some smoke. It smelled bitter next to Uglo's Italian cheroot. Like my last remark.

"You got all the answers, Dime," Uglo said, taking the cheroot out of his mouth for the first time since he lit it. "Tell me some of what you and your buddy was talking over the other night. That is, apart from how tough you were on the Normandy beaches."

"It was a private matter and that's how I am going to keep it."

Uglo put the cheroot back in his mouth. Immediately the ash slipped off in a long, thin roll. Some landed on his vest, some on his necktie. He lifted his hand and absently brushed at it once or twice without much success. But tobacco ash didn't worry a cop from Okie City. Compared to corn feed and horse shit it probably looked distinguished.

"That's your privilege," he said. "Till someone makes a snatch you don't have to say a thing. But get this. I may only be around this town a short while, but pinching the killer of this boy is on my sheet, and I don't want any dick with vengeance on his mind getting in the way."

"You're the corniest thing since Sad Sack," I said. "As for revenge, I hadn't given it a thought until you mentioned it. But it wouldn't be a bad way to spend my declining years. Come to think of it, there are worse objectives in life."

The room had become warm and stuffy, like the air before a storm. It didn't seem to bother Uglo. He just sat there, listening. He looked used to heat; probably wore a wool undershirt the year through. Probably the same one.

"Call me corny, Dime," Uglo said. "But I don't get paid to think up smart conversation." He got up off his chair very slowly. Like a cowpoke after a month in the saddle.

Some lights flickered on over a few tables at the front of the room, and above our heads a wall fan began to whirr. Its head moved slowly from side to side, slower than an octogenarian watching a tennis match.

Uglo looked down at me over his mustache, over the butt of his Italian cheroot.

"Save your funny lines for the people who think cops are the guys who direct traffic—the smart dames with too much nothing on their minds and less under their petticoats. Your kind of customers. That kind are your problem, Dime. But catching killers is my job. Step one foot out of line and I'll have you picked up faster than a pimp on Fifth Avenue."

There was a stiff silence when he finished. Then I said, "Okay, captain, I'll play it your way. A client of mine had a husband who lost a briefcase that didn't belong to him. I was going to find it. That's all. Pozo was going to help me nose around. Maybe his death is connected in some way. Maybe it was a coincidence. It does happen, you know."

"All too often," Uglo said.

I didn't believe what I was saying and neither did Uglo. But we kept up the charade. It was a lot easier than sticking me in the can and giving me the third degree.

"Just so you can sleep nice and easy," I said, "I'll keep clean as a nurse's bib. And for good measure I won't shoot moose or G-men out of season. But if you don't pick up the gun that murdered Pozo before they ship you back home, I'll make finding him my one and only ambition."

"That's providing someone isn't stuffing you into a pine box," the policeman said. Then Uglo did something with his mouth that looked like a smile. But I wouldn't have known about that. It wasn't something I had seen a policeman do before.

"You missed your vocation, shamus," he said, taking the dead stump of the cheroot from between his lips. "You should have been Joe Louis's punching bag."

He let the smoked cheroot fall to the floor.

"He sure as eggs would've knocked the crap outa you."

"Sure as eggs," I said.

Captain Uglo from Oklahoma City, on transfer to the Philadelphia City Police Department, took an antique pocket watch from the left-hand pocket of his vest and made a far-sighted inspection. He patted his belly, sighed and put the timepiece away.

"Gone and missed lunch," he said. "Time has just flown

by talking with yourself, and it being so informative and all. If I wander back to HQ, type out my report and make a few inquiries I might just grab supper before lights-out. It doesn't ever pay to work on an empty stomach. Believe me. It makes a man lose his sense of humor."

Uglo turned and waddled loosely toward the door. The uniformed cop was still waiting where I had left him, by the top table. He still had his hands on his hips. When Uglo drew level he stiffened and said something. Uglo nodded and the uniformed man waved a hand to Max Slovan who was busy messing with a cue-tip and some glue. The two policemen pushed through the swinging doors and a trickle of men made their way into the room. One by one, lights flickered over the pool tables.

I didn't leave for some time. I just sat, looking every so often at the line of balls, at the chalk mark of Joey Pozo's hand and his finger pointing to them.

Pool balls are colored in two sets, half striped, the others spotted. There are fifteen all told, including a black eight ball. Each ball has a number as well as an individual color. I took out my notebook and made a diagram of the line of balls. There was a main group and then one ball, number 13, on its own. The numbers on the main group of balls, in sequence, were: 12, 9, 14, 7, 3, 6, 7, 15, 1, 4.

The balls numbered 3, 6 and 7 and the numbers 1 and 4 were bunched together. The others had about a two-inch gap on either side.

I didn't know what it all meant, but I knew no game of pool that used such a combination.

I hauled myself off the chair and lit another cigarette.

Then I made a note of the sequence of balls and put the note in my pocket. For the first time in a millennium of despair I saw a chink of hope.

By late afternoon the sky cleared completely to let a warm fall sun shine brightly over the city. Its fading brilliance glowed with an elderly dignity among the tree-lined avenues and tidy squares. Fairmount Park was clogged with the golds and Titian reds of maple trees, their dense foliage rocking gracefully in the faintest of breezes.

Amber sunlight fell through my office window and was too bright and too warm. I pulled down the venetian blind and scrambled the thick beam into neat horizontal strips of light and shade.

Max told me that Joey Pozo had fixed up for an all-night game that was to be a strictly no-spectators affair. The room closed officially at eleven-thirty, at which time Max had phoned for a cab, giving Joey the spare set of keys to lock up. It was odd, Max admitted, that no spectators were to be allowed, but some hustlers preferred to play that way. There was no one in the poolroom at the time Max left, except for Joey who was, it seems, spending a lot of time on the phone. When Max arrived the following morning he found the doors open and the keys still in Joey Pozo's pocket. Of course, with hindsight the business about the spectators was nothing more than a set-up to keep the meeting private.

With a bullet from a .38 in the stomach, Joey would have died slowly. He would have instinctively put his hands to the wound and they would have been covered with blood. Dumped on the table, and without legs, he would have been helpless. I was sure that Ratenner had no part in Pozo's death or in the shoot-out at Luigi's Dine and Dance. I was sure about it in the way I was sure that the pool balls were placed in a line deliberately, prior to Joey Pozo being shot. There was no way in which he could have touched them after and not left a trace of blood.

I started to look for the phone directory. There was one once but I couldn't find it anywhere. I owned a 1939 Packard convertible with a worn transmission shaft, a soft-brimmed hat, a fawn gabardine raincoat, a full bottle of Jim Beam, a gun, an overdraft, a powerful imagination, a weakness for women of all ages between seventeen and forty-five and a private investigator's license issued by Philadelphia City Hall. But I didn't own a phone directory. Finally I came to the conclusion that I had either pawned it or fed it to the mice. But I needed a phone book then, in a hurry. And that meant a trip along the hall to my neighbor: Heinrich Zoftig, junior partner of H. and H. Zoftig and Company, Wholesalers in Costume Jewelry and the Meanest Man on Earth.

On the way I popped over to the window, just to make sure Ratenner's boys hadn't fallen down on their job. I made scissors with two fingers, stuck them between two slats of the venetian blind and peered through the thin gap. The two men in the Pontiac had rolled back the hood and were parked on the sunny side of the street. They were both hidden under dark glasses and doing their best to enjoy the last of the sun. One man had taken off his jacket and the other was smoking lazily with his head resting on the back of the seat.

Tempus fugit, I reminded myself and took me and my smile along to borrow old man Zoftig's phone directory. I also took my gun for protection and the lease of my office in case he asked for a deposit.

His office door was the universal frosted glass square in a piece of stained timber. Under the glass a sign said WALK IN. It was an invitation that was not, as experience had shown, extended to me. Zoftig was forever making complaints to the landlord about guns going off in the middle of the afternoon and stiffs cluttering up their doorway. But a lot of that was his Gestapo-like imagination. It was true that once I shot a client who thought I was becoming too intimate with his estranged wife and who had come after me with an ax, but I only shot him in the leg. It was true that the client fell through Zoftig's door and spilled a lot of blood over his office carpet before smashing the place up with his ax. It was also true that once or twice desperate clients have behaved unconventionally, like the estranged wife of the client I shot in the leg. She came to my office, took off her clothes and paraded naked up and down the hall until I withdrew my threat not to see her again. Her name, I recall, was Mrs. Body.

I knocked once and didn't bother waiting for a reply. Although he looked it, old man Zoftig wasn't so old: no more than fifty-five. He stood over six feet in his socks and stooped badly, like a hockey stick. He was all bones, covered in a heavy woolen suit and a shirt with a starched collar. His head was extremely bald and an unpleasant liverish yellow. His nose was long and his ears big and thin-skinned, almost transparent. His mouth was cruel and mean and closed tight over a hundred bucks' worth of gold fillings.

He was standing beside a very old, highly polished oak roll-topped desk.

His mother, whom he lived with, was sitting by the window, looking out. She was a smaller, fatter version of her son. With hair.

"Get out of here, you sonovabitch," old man Zoftig shouted in a thick German accent as I entered. "You want to shoot someone, go someplace else. Or maybe you want shoot my mudder? Go ahead, shoot."

"Heinrich, Heinrich," Mrs. Zoftig said. "Your heart, remember."

She was eating a lot of something on pumpernickel—cabbage and chicken liver and cream cheese. And there was more food on the desk, including a sausage as thick as a drainpipe and black as an old dried prune. Old man Zoftig was busily circumcising it with a bone-handled pocket knife.

Mrs. Zoftig wiped a smudge of food out of the corner of her mouth with a fleshy middle finger. She waggled it with some agitation at the sausage. Her son speared a slice which she grabbed greedily from the tip of the knife and began chewing like someone with dentures eating a lump of candy.

All the time I had been in the room old man Zoftig had not taken his sharp little eyes off me for a second.

"Trouble," he said aggressively, and sliced a fat lump off the end of the black sausage. "Ven you valk in the door it means trouble. Instead of messink vis naked ladies and shooting up the neighborhood, try selling paste brooches vis high-class vorkmanship to people who vant cheap from the Japs. Trouble ve got already. Take yours outa here."

Mrs. Zoftig shrugged her shoulders under a blue woolen shawl and brushed some more food off her lap with a few deft slaps from the back of her hand.

"He vants the phone book," she said. Her voice was thin and crackly. "Give him, Heinrich, *um Gottes willin*."

Old man Zoftig's face turned a nasty color and his mouth got even thinner. It was the thinnest thing outside a crack in an oil painting by Vermeer.

He rocked slightly on his heels and clenched his fists. Lending me the phone book was never going to be easy. He said, "Bring it back the minute you finish, you sonovabitch." Then he opened a drawer in the desk and began the slow and painfully deliberate search, picking up wads of paper as if he expected something unpleasant to jump out and bite him, like a poisonous spider or a small shark.

There wasn't a lot of room in Zoftig's office. Rows of small cardboard boxes were piled from the floor to the ceiling. On the front of each box there was a sample of the contents, stitched on with heavy-duty cotton. A lot of the stuff was quite pretty in an old-fashioned, turn-of-the-century way. But most of the styles had gone with lace and crinoline.

At last Zoftig found the book and thumped it on the edge of the desk. It made dust.

"Take," he said, through a bared set of black teeth and gold nuggets. "Take and go."

Over the desk was a large trade calendar with a picture of a smiling *fraulein* with flaxen hair tied in bright red ribbons and eyes the color of blue ice. She was holding a jewel-studded goblet foaming with a light beer, and she wore earrings the size of chandeliers. A brooch of pearls no bigger than a turnip was pinned strategically on the tip of her right breast, which was climbing, with its generously proportioned companion, over the edge of a low-cut evening gown.

I tucked the book under my arm and smiled back at the girl on the calendar.

Old man Zoftig's sharp eyes caught my gaze.

"Sex-mad Americans," he hissed under his breath.

"Many thanks," I said to dead ears and hearts with no love for me, and backed carefully out of their office, closing the door gently behind me.

On a quiet night the sound of Mrs. Zoftig eating carried all the way to Marconi Plaza, eight blocks away.

27

The patch of sunlit bars was still on my office floor, but a little paler. I stepped over them and sat down at my desk.

It was time to do some work.

I put the phone book neatly in front of me, tore off the used sheet of paper from the top of my scratch pad and picked up a blunt-nosed pencil. I stuck the end into the pencil sharpener and swung the small handle a few times. The blades ground noisily over a long curly shaving. The faint smell of sweet wood hit my nose, and the dry smell of carbon. I laid the sharpened pencil beside the pad and got out the list of numbers I had made from the balls on Joey Pozo's table. I placed the piece of crumpled paper on the pad and smoothed it flat. I then took a bottle from my desk and poured a finger of whiskey very carefully into a paper cup from the water cooler.

I was just about ready. I drank the finger and poured out another. I was ready.

I drew eleven circles representing the balls and filled them with the figures. There was no doubt in my mind that Joey Pozo had presented me with a coded message. I only hoped it was simple.

The simplest code I knew was numerical and alphabetical. The easiest information Joey Pozo could have supplied was a phone number. I started there. With about a hundred million phones in America there was a chance that, assuming it was a phone number, I might strike lucky.

The first number was twelve, which represented the letter L. The second number gave me an I, the third N, and the fourth G. So far so good. The next numbers were slightly separate, in a group of three. They made the word LINGCFK. I didn't need a phone book to tell me there was no exchange with a name remotely like that, not outside Russia at least. I did the sums with the remaining balls and got the whole word. It was LINGCFKOADM. The A and D were also grouped together and the M a long way from the others. I suspected there was a reason for this, which I had missed. For a local phone number seven of the eleven balls would represent figures. But the problem was that four of the balls were double figures, which gave me sixteen numbers. I was getting nowhere.

I poured out some more Jim Beam, drank some and let it warm my gums before swallowing it. I put a line through the word on the pad and thought some more about the grouped balls. Maybe I would get something by adding them up. I lit a cigarette, rested it on the ashtray under the desk light and was just doing the total when there was a knock on the door of the outer office. I looked at my watch. It showed a quarter after four.

He was not especially tall but he walked with assurance, like someone who was at ease in the company of both men and women. He was wearing a belted camel hair wrap coat. It looked good on him. His face was deeply tanned, square with dark brown wavy hair that smelled nice. He had a thin mustache and uncluttered hazel eyes. His mouth was easy to look at and I imagined it had an easy way with words. It was smiling.

"My name is Teddy Holland," he said as if it mattered more to me than him. Next he took a card from his wallet, placed it with more show than was necessary on my desk and looked at the client's chair.

"May I sit down?"

I picked up the card. Just the name; nothing more.

"Help yourself, Mr. Holland," I said. "What can I do for you?"

He smiled a second time and leaned back in the chair,

a wobbly old thing that I had grown fond of. It didn't worry him. He took out a cigarette case as big as a paperback and stuck a cigarette between his lips. He had a fat gold ring on the fourth finger of his left hand, and the cuffs of his shirt were held together by more gold. Teddy Holland had the sweet face of Hollywood and the sharp clothes of Chicago. Normally you didn't see them together.

"Actually," he said, lighting up, "I am here on behalf of your client, Elaine Damone." He let out some smoke and waited. His eyes looked hard at mine and didn't flinch, even when I stopped staring back. I poured out some more Jim Beam and held up the bottle.

"Drink?" I said.

He nodded. "Sure," he said. "Just make it the one. I am a little pressed."

He gave his wristwatch a quick couple of winds to emphasize the point.

I poured a second cup half full and placed it on the edge of the desk. Holland looked at it, took it and stuck it under his nose. He smiled again and sipped the hooch. He didn't cough.

"You said you came here on behalf of Elaine Damone," I said, and did some smiling myself. Just to show I could.

Holland let some ash drop onto the floor and nodded. "She would have telephoned you or dropped by herself but she's been unexpectedly called away. On business. That's why I am here. She trusts me with a great many of her confidences."

There was a pause while we both took a drag on our cigarettes and downed a little liquor.

"To get to the point, Dime," Holland said, "the matter concerning her brother, Stanton, is no longer one that requires your assistance. Professional or otherwise. Elaine hoped that you would not consider her action as in any way being a reflection on yourself or your work. Her reason for the decision is simply that the matter has been resolved without a further financial transaction having taken place. The items that belonged to Stanton Damone have been returned and subsequently destroyed. That is all there is to say. I hope you understand."

"Shouldn't tax my powers of concentration too much," I said.

"Fine," Holland said, and we both smiled at the same time.

He got up with the manner of a job well done and stubbed his cigarette on the carpet with the right toe of one of his new shoes.

"Oh, by the way," he said, "Elly—that is, Elaine—asked me to give you this." He took an envelope from the inside pocket of his jacket. "It's another day's pay. A hundred dollars. There is also a generous estimate of your expenses. You will find five hundred dollars in all."

He threw the envelope onto my desk, next to the notes I had been making.

"In addition," Holland said, his eyes narrowing. "It is hoped that four hundred dollars will be seen as an indication that you will not make any future contact with Elaine and erase all record of ever having met her. That is imperative. It is also, if you like, part of my business."

"What's your other part?" I said. "Just for the record I am about to destroy."

"I am an adviser," he said. "People pay me to advise them."

"Would you advise me to take any notice of what you just told me?"

"For free," he said. "I most certainly would."

I picked up the envelope, cut it open and let four one-hundred-dollar bills float onto the desk.

"I don't like quitting, Mr. Holland," I said. "It's bad for trade. For morale. My business isn't bursting at the seams but I get by. If it gets out that I quit on a job, or was taken off it . . ."

"Okay, okay," Holland said. "Turn off the tap. How much do you want to close the deal? I assume that's what you are leading up to."

"You assume wrong." I stood up. I was slightly taller.

He was slightly wider. "What I am saying is that I don't think much of your explanation. It might be Miss Damone's but I don't like it and I don't believe it. Blackmailers don't quit till they've bled you drier than dust. I don't want your money, Mr. Holland. I don't know what I want. It's just that picking up five centuries for not even having to wag my big toe leaves a bitter taste in my mouth."

Holland moved a step nearer.

"That's not the way I heard it. Miss Damone's housegirl told me she was under the impression that you waggled one hell of a lot more than your big toe."

He wasn't smiling when he said that and his fists were clenched. Just a little.

I sat down again, to take the heat off. I didn't think Teddy Holland would smack me while I was sitting down. I didn't think he would smack me while I was standing up, or any other way. I got the feeling it was all show. I said, "I wouldn't believe everything Orientals tell you. Inscrutable they may be, but the ones I've met can't tell a tall story from a short one."

Holland let that go.

"Just stay away from Elaine and you will probably live to a ripe old age," he said. "Mess with her and you mess with me. And that, like I said, is not advisable."

He gave me a smile to end all smiles.

"Besides," he went on, "Elaine tells me you are very busy on another case. She thought you would be anxious to get on with that. I realize it is none of my business, but I would endorse her considerate observation."

His eyes dropped to my scratch pad. Then he said, "Sorry if I sounded a little high-handed, Dime. Only this whole blackmail thing has had everyone jumpy."

"Sure," I said. I turned the scratch pad around so he could read what I had written and crossed out.

"Any good at puzzles?"

Holland's eyes widened.

"The case I am working on," I said. "It all means something."

"Nothing to me," Holland said. "Sorry."

"I think I went wrong with the three numbers grouped together. I have a hunch they should be added to make one number and not seen as singles."

"So it's some kind of code?" Holland said, running a manicured fingernail along the bottom of his mustache.

"That's the size of it," I said. "It was worked out by an ex-ranger I met in the war. He was a wireless op."

"Interesting," Holland said, and sounded it.

I picked up the pencil.

"On the other hand, some of the figures might need to be separated. What I am after, I think, is nothing more than a phone number or possibly even a place. A house name or a hotel. Something of that order."

"Very interesting."

"Very," I said. "But don't let me keep you. You said you were pressed."

"Oh, yes," Holland said, and did his last smile of the afternoon. "I am glad we have come to an understanding, Dime. Glad for Elaine's sake. She is a very extraordinary woman."

He held out a tanned hand and I shook it.

I heard his footsteps die away down the hall and the clank of the self-operating elevator doors. I waited a minute, then went to the window. The sun had almost sunk. I let up the venetian blind and noticed that the puddle under the window ledge had all but dried. There was just a dark patch the shape of Long Island. But not so big.

I saw Holland leave the building, cross the street and flag down a cab. He didn't drive a car and didn't wear a hat. So much for Teddy Holland. So much for Ratenner's boys. They were nowhere to be seen.

I sat down at my desk once more and got busy. First I picked up the five hundred-dollar bills Elaine Damone had given me and put them in a manila envelope. I wrote Philadelphia's branch of the Veterans' Association on the front and stuck on a picture of Roosevelt. I put the envelope in my pocket, opened the phone book and jotted down an address: Eckard Avenue, Abington.

Joey Pozo's code was easy once I separated the number of the first ball and added up the middle three. The name I got was Abington M. M could have meant anything, but I was sure as malted milk it stood for Motel. There was no phone listing for that name, and the alternatives that had an M ending were the Abington Mortuary and Abington Meat Suppliers. If I was wrong about the motel I would at least be in the right place to check out the others.

I put some bullets in my gun, in case things got hot, and folded my raincoat over my arm, in case the weather got cold. The last thing I did before shutting up shop was to have another peep at Teddy Holland's visiting card. I picked it up and pressed my thumb over his name.

The ink was so fresh it smudged.

28

Saturday night. Traffic was coming from out of town and I made swift progress north along Broad Street. I pushed on hard past City Hall, to where the road becomes Highway 611, and pushed harder still as the dusk took hold of the Philadelphia suburbs of Ogontz, La Mott and Cedarbrook. Some of the houses I passed were splendid. Some were less than splendid and some were just houses. A lot of the older architecture showed signs that the Wall Street collapse and the last war had both taken a bite. Once fine lawns were overgrown and once proud porches swayed on rotten wood. But most places would only need a coat of paint to put a smile back on a real estate agent's face.

It was almost dark when I drove through two brick pillars and a rusty iron gate. The place may have been worth checking into at one time. Fashionable people might have put it in their address books and told their friends. But all that would have been back in the twenties. No one would want to stay there now. There was just too much flaked paint. Too much stale, weary air.

The driveway was coated with black tire marks and dotted with patches of glistening sump oil. And there was an ugly-looking evergreen with a welcome sign nailed carelessly to its trunk. I nearly overshot the turn-off. If I had, the Packard would have bounced down three paved steps and into a smelly swimming pool thick with slimy green water and decomposing leaves.

The motel building was an open-fronted square, the east and west wings supported by strong iron posts, like those on a pier. A decorated cast-iron walkway ran along the inside of the flat-roofed apartments. They were all evenly divided, with one door and two windows each. Most of the windows were unlit and the portes cocheres beneath were mainly empty. The central building was two stories high and overlooked the deep end of the swimming pool. Four post lights with dull, domed metal shades stood at each corner of the pool. There was also a dull glow on the other side of an open, sliding glass door that was to one side of reception.

I turned right at an overblown rose bush and parked under the end apartment on the left side of the building, reversing first so I faced the exit.

I got out of the car, put the top down, left the keys in the dash and the door unlocked. All that would help if I had to leave in a hurry.

There was music. The comb-and-paper reeds and honey-pot brass of Glenn Miller's band wafted out from the glass door. The sound bounced off the walls of the two wings, creating an echo like you get in very large, very empty men's rooms.

I walked through the porte cochere and then along the side of the pool. My footsteps sounded unusually heavy, sharp and clunking, as if I were shod with steel-capped diving boots.

Frogs lived in the pool, which was rimmed with a raised wall about a foot high. The top of the wall was sunken to hold a flower bed. But there wasn't much worth pruning or watering. Just some moss and a few dead ferns.

As I approached the curved steel rail of the steps, there was a series of faint plops and the surface of the water rippled with tiny, exploding bubbles. Dark shapes the color of wet stones kicked into the murky, silent, shadowy depths. To safety.

Lucky old frogs.

There was a woman standing against the open door from where the music was blaring. She had a drink in her hand and a voice in her throat. She held the drink like a barfly and used her voice like a circus barker.

"Come over here, good looking, and meet Masie Webster."

She was in her late forties and her figure was spreading faster than spilled milk. A lot of her was almost into a peg-top velveteen skirt with slits that were too long and a frothy organdy blouse that needed buttoning. She was the second woman in a week that I had met who didn't wear a brassiere. Her face was the color of uncooked bread, her lips were large and puffy and painted with less care than drunks count change. The shade of lipstick she was using was no brighter than a pink neon light. She had been doing something with her hair. It was piled high and dyed bright yellow. The style looked good on Ann Sheridan but on La Webster it looked like a heap of rope and was as attractive as scorched straw. Her eyebrows had been plucked and were scribbled over with thin pencil. Her stockings had a pair of wobbly seams and covered a pair of wobbly legs. She was barefoot.

She leaned provocatively against the frame of the sliding door, put her hand on her hip and said, "You a beer or whiskey man?" She lunged forward and grabbed my arm, partly to steady herself, partly to drag me into her room.

She dragged me into her room.

It's commonly said that dogs grow to look like their owners. Masie Webster didn't have a dog. She had a room and it was every inch the mess she was. It hadn't made up its mind whether to be a bar, a den, an office or a boudoir. There were features and furniture from all. Mostly it looked like a storage room.

What light there was came from a tiny, peach-tinted tube over the wall mirror of a mirror-fronted bar and from a small table lamp on a large, leather-topped desk. You could just see a hand in front of your face.

An undistinguished secretary was jammed full of box files and a near-luminous acid green studio couch was piled high with soft frilly cushions in a mixture of polka dots. In the middle of the far wall stood a Victrola Golden Throat radio phonograph—a collection of tubes, knobs and wires stuffed into a mock Hepplewhite walnut cabinet. It cost over four hundred bucks and sounded like it.

"Didn't catch your name," Masie Webster said, and threw me down on the studio couch.

The record came to an end with a few clicks. The machine automatically fed another onto the turntable.

"Mike Dime," I said quickly, before the next platter killed the silence.

"Nice," she said. "Let me get you something strong."

She added a wink that was meant to make me feel at home. It would have scared off a plague.

More Miller magic swooned through the speaker. Masie Webster got herself over to the bar, emptied half a bottle of Wild Turkey bourbon into a beer glass and headed back in my direction. On the way she turned out the table lamp.

"Too darn bright in here," she said.

"A little loud as well," I said cheerily.

"Gotcha," she said. "Can't hear a darn thing."

She gave me the glass and fiddled with a couple of the knobs on the Victrola and finally got the decibels to a level that civilized people could talk over.

"Love music," she said. "Simply love it."

She wiggled her large hips out of time with the music and spilled some booze from the glass in her hand. She had cheap-looking rings on every painted finger, and both arms ended in gaudy rhinestone bracelets that rattled like chattering teeth.

The big toe of her left foot was poking through her nylon stocking. A long time ago it had been painted the same red as her fingernails.

"Danced professionally," she said. "Top-class hoofer. New York to Honolulu. Straight ballet to chorus. You name it, Masie Webster danced it."

The music hit a riff. Masie Webster kicked a leg at my nose and waved her free hand wildly. She closed her eyes and opened her mouth.

"Let's have it again, honey," she yelled. "I do love music."

The trance lasted to the end of the record. Then she stopped kicking and wiggling and came and sat down with a lot of gasping next to me on the studio couch. She landed like a Lancaster bomber.

"Jeez," she said. "Those boys can really blow."

Another record plopped onto the stack. More Miller. More smooch. "Met Mr. Webster on the floor," she said. "God bless his late departed soul." Large damp patches were spreading under her arms. She took a small lace-edged handkerchief from under the sleeve of her blouse and wiped her bare neck down to the cleavage.

"Darn hot," she said. "Have a refill, buster."

I said I was doing fine.

"Poor Wilbur," she said. "That's him on the desk." She pointed through the gloom to a ten-by-eight in a walnut frame. There wasn't much of him.

"He bought it in Guam," Masie Webster said vacantly. "July 26, nineteen hundred and forty-four." She threw back what was left in her glass. "Drink up, lover boy," she said, putting her hand on my knee. "And tell Masie Webster what she can do for you."

I sipped a little from my glass, but made it look more.

I smacked my lips and said, "I am in the investigation business, looking for a guy who I think maybe's staying here at present, or stayed here during the last few days."

"A cop," Masie Webster said.

"Private," I said. I took out my license and held it under her nose.

"That's nice," she said without reading it.

I got out a pack of cigarettes, gave one to Masie Webster and put another in the corner of my mouth. I let her light them both with a fat-bellied Ronson table lighter that she had dragged from a long coffee table made from the split trunk of a redwood tree. We blew smoke away from each other's faces.

"It's like this, Mrs. Webster," I said. "I think the man I am looking for could be wounded and possibly dangerous. He may also have registered under a false name. I was wondering if I could cast an eye on your register?"

"Phooey," she said. "You're too good-looking to be a cop. Drink up that corn juice and then we'll dance a little."

It was going to be tougher than I thought.

I sipped some more and put on my Macy's Santa Claus smile.

"The trouble is," I said. "I am kind of short of time."

Masie Webster took the hat off my head and hurled it like a discus into the corner of the room.

"What's time between friends?"

She pulled my head toward her and stuck a very wet, gin-soaked kiss on my lips.

"That's for bein' a good boy," she said. "Now take off your jacket and we'll dance. I've got some red-hot stuff somewhere. Wilbur, God rest his soul, was jazz crazy. Got 'em all, and red-hot, every one."

She got up, went to the bar, filled up, opened a large oak box, pulled out a handful of gramophone records, dropped some on the carpeted floor and did a flat-footed samba back to the couch.

"Here," she said. "Look through these while I go and get into something I can dance in. This damn skirt restricts a girl's movements."

"Fine," I said, putting the records down. "Why don't I pop over to the reception desk to check out the register while you're doing that and we'll spin a little later?"

She was standing with her drink to her lips. She took the drink away and leaned unsteadily over me.

"'Cause I might need some help getting out of this darn skirt, buster. That's why. It fits tighter than a goddamn noose."

Masie Webster straightened up and turned around. She dug her finger at the zip that ran to the base of her rump.

"Close those sweet eyes of yours and make a start," she said. "Just unhook me and nature will do the rest."

I stood up just as she fell down. I caught her, but the worst way a man can. My hand accidentally sank into her breasts, like talons into prey. They felt heavy and bloated, like a cow's udder feels when the milkmaid takes the day off. As we both fell backwards the side slit in Masie Webster's skirt ripped apart and some thigh came out for air. It hung over the top of her nylons like vanilla ice cream over a cone.

"Easy, lover boy," she shrieked. "Let a girl get undressed first, for chrissakes."

I had fallen half onto the floor, half onto the couch. My

right elbow landed in a pile of Benny Goodmans and my left knee was somewhere between Masie Webster's legs.

I think I must have said sorry because she said, "You better be, soldier. You goddamn better be. This outfit cost me eleven bucks." She struggled to lift herself.

"I'm through with this game, buster. Don't like the way it turned out. You can pack yourself off. Masie Webster can do without perverts."

Somehow she managed to disentangle herself, rolled over and got on her hands and knees, the torn front flap of her skirt hanging from her waist like a long, black, tattered flag.

"I've met your type," she snarled. "Coming in here and taking advantage."

I smiled without too much conviction and tried to get it good-tempered, I said something passive, but I knew I was drifting out, losing sight of land, watching sanity fade in the mists of Masie Webster's fantasies. I knew what I had to do and knew it would have to be done soon.

"Think we better have some law down here," she said.

Sooner the better.

Before Masie Webster could utter another sound I lurched across the carpet extending my fist ahead of me, like a ram, and hit her chin. It wasn't a hard blow—more of a clip. She gurgled, then collapsed on her face, her arms and legs giving out like broken stilts.

I crawled toward the prostrate woman and checked her condition. She was colder than a nun's kiss. I got up off the floor and went to the bar. I found what she had been drinking and emptied it onto the floor beside her. I put the bottle in her hand. Then I picked up my glass, wiped it and put it back on the mirrored bar. Then I remembered Masie Webster had hurled my hat somewhere. I cursed and wasted valuable time hunting around for it. After ten minutes' solid searching I found it in the large oak box where Wilbur Webster had lovingly filed his collection of 78s. There were some fine recordings of all kinds. On another evening, in another world, me and Wilbur could have run over the rarities, puffing our pipes and tippling our scotch and tapping our feet. It was all there in his box, everything from Enrico Caruso to Eddie Condon. I dressed my head and noticed Dinu Lipatti was sitting where my hat had been. He was playing Bach, "Jesu, Joy of Man's Desiring." I picked it up, padded to the Victrola, stepping over Masie Webster, snoring as happy as a sow feeding piglets, and slipped the disc onto the spindle in the center of the turntable.

I lowered the automatic release arm and set the switch to constant replay. Then I turned the starter button and the wax dropped onto the spinning turntable. Jerkily the pick-up arm cranked up, across and down onto the clear rim of the record. Scratches gave way to music.

It was the sound of angels weeping.

The Abington Motel register didn't tell me much, except that a lot of couples called Smith and Jones had stopped over on their way to and from each other's wives and husbands.

The last three days had seen the names of two new guests. Father Dooley O'Hanrahan was in Room Eight and someone with a signature like a doctor's prescription was in Room Nine. All the other rooms were empty. The last guest to check out did so a week before the election, eleven days ago.

I walked uneasily by the side of the pool and looked up at Rooms Eight and Nine. The man I wanted was in one of them. I crossed to the opposite side of the pool and checked the rooms for light. The priest's room was dark, the other lit. That meant nothing. The priest could be asleep, or praying, or he could be just another Mr. Smith having fun.

The walkway ran along all three sides of the above-ground floors and could be reached from both inside and outside the building. I climbed the outside steps, which were cast like a honeycomb and noisy underfoot. I kept rubber overshoes in the trunk of the Packard but I had messed around long enough. Ratenner wanted his briefcase in less than ten hours and it was going to take every minute of that.

I crept around the three sides to Room Nine, which was the last but one on the wing opposite to where I had parked. First I put an ear close to the door where the priest was staying. It sounded the way empty rooms sound. Empty. I ducked under the first lit window, passed the door, crept under the second window and then straightened up. The only sound I made came from my creaking bones. Both windows had curtains and they were both drawn. They were too thick to see through. But the second window's curtains did not quite reach the ledge. There was a gap of maybe an inch, enough to get a glimpse of the layout and possibly the occupant. I dropped down to a crouch and peered through the brightly lit slit.

The bed was facing the window and was the only thing I could see clearly. That wasn't so bad because there was someone on it. Someone I wanted. His crossed feet were in cheap, dark brown socks and his legs were lazing in a pair of crumpled serge pants the color of soot. His jacket was draped across the back of the bedside chair and a cigarette was burning under a curl of gray smoke in a metal ashtray advertising Coca-Cola on the seat of the chair. There was a night table with some medical stuff, rolls of bandages, Vaseline, ointment and some other things used to dress wounds. There was also a bottle of Canadian Club, which was half empty. The man had undone his tie, unbuttoned his shirt and was reading a picture magazine, holding it by the top, his right arm level with his head. The magazine blocked his face and I could not see his left arm. It seemed to be covered by something like a sling.

I slipped my hand into my clothing and pulled out my gun. I released the safety catch and waited. The man on the bed came to the end of the page and put the magazine down, picked up the cigarette and pulled hard. Then he put down the smoke, poured a slug from the tall bottle of whiskey and left the full glass on the night table. He did this so he could turn the page of the magazine. He couldn't do two things at once, at least not with his hands. The bullet hole in his left shoulder had caused the blood to freeze up the muscles, to form a natural splint, stopping the arm from too much movement so the wound could heal efficiently.

The bullet that disabled the man before me came from the gun I was holding. My bullet. My gun. My man.

I had seen the face several times. I had seen it at Slovan's the time I spoke to Joey Pozo. Then at the Dine and Dance.

I had called the man the Shadow, but he had another name. He was a small-time canary, a petty larcenist and general nobody called Olly Keppard.

Still crouching, I stretched out my arm and tapped the door twice with the barrel of my gun. Keppard jumped up and shot his good hand under his pillow. When it came out there was a gun the same as mine clenched tightly in his fist.

"Hold it," he said. "Who's there?"

His face was very gray and his long chin thick with stubble, almost a beard. His eyebrows were high and fiercely curved at the outside edges and deeply dented where they almost met at the top of a beaky nose. He looked like a hawk who'd run out of shaving soap. He swiveled his slender frame off the bed and took up a position outside my range of vision.

I said nothing.

"Who is it?" he said again. His voice was nearer the door.

"Father O'Hanrahan," I said warmly, in a nice, rounded Irish brogue. For all I knew, Keppard and O'Hanrahan were old pals. For all I knew, O'Hanrahan could have been a Chinaman.

"Who?" Keppard said a third time.

I made some scuffling sounds and braced my back against the rail of the walkway.

"'Tis the priest from next door," I said.

"So what?" the voice behind the door growled, a little puzzled. "I'm busy."

"And I am locked out," I said. "I need a little kindness."

Olly Keppard made some noises with his throat and mumbled something under his breath. "I got a cranked arm," he said. "Find someone else."

"Sure and there is no one but yourself," I croaked like Barry Fitzgerald with an onion up his shirt. "It only needs an extra shove," I said insistently.

There was a pause.

"Okay, okay," he said. "But I ain't no locksmith."

I heard the key click in the lock and the door opened no wider than it needed to let a snake out. But it was wide enough for me. I lifted my leg high, bringing my thigh up almost to my chest. Then I kicked with all the power I had. The impact sent Keppard reeling across the room and the door off one of its hinges. As Keppard hit the far wall he fired his gun, but not at me. The arm that held the weapon was pointed at the ceiling and the bullet boomed into the plaster. The room was lit by a wall light and a too bright center bulb. That popped out and the place went dim, like a theater before the curtain goes up. I leaped toward Keppard and swung another foot. The toe of my shoe hit his wrist and his .38 sailed into the air like it had been suddenly, carelessly discarded. Keppard's eyes were sick as he screamed out. He was in a lot of pain. And that was only the beginning.

"Remember me?" I said and kicked him in the stomach, "Mike Dime. The big sucker from Tasker Street."

He groaned and saliva trickled from the corner of his mouth. He fell on his wounded arm and immediately blood began to seep through the dressing. It was a dark red, almost brown.

I kicked him again.

He called me a bastard and lost consciousness. I put away my gun. I wasn't going to need it.

The air in the room was heavy and stale, thick with cigarette smoke and the sharp tang of antiseptic. The right-hand wall was mostly a walk-in closet and the left, a partitioned shower room and bathroom. The furniture was old and solid, just enough for the needs of two people. But there was no one sleeping in the second bed. It was not even made up. I opened the sliding door of the bathroom and looked for something large to put water in. There was a toothbrush mug on a glass shelf with no toothbrush. I trudged back into the bedroom and picked up the metal wastebasket, emptied the trash onto the carpet and tried to fill the can up from the sink. It didn't fit, so instead I filled it with cold water from the shower nozzle. I then walked with the can of water to the only easy chair in the bedroom, picked up a bundle of Dick Tracy comics and a few copies of the *Saturday Evening Post* from the seat and eased into it. I put down the can and lit a Camel. I looked at Keppard for a while, expecting something to happen. Like feeling pity, or anger. Nothing did happen. So with the cigarette still hanging from my mouth I hurled the water in Olly Keppard's face. He moved an inch and his eyelids flickered like the wings of a dying moth. A lot of blood was pouring from the wound in his arm and a lot of pain was racing through his body. I got up out of the chair and went over to the bottle of Canadian Club. I pulled out the stop, leaned over Keppard and rammed the spout into his mouth. Some blood ran along the neck of the bottle. I pushed the bottle upright and almost emptied it.

Very slowly Keppard's eyes opened and he began to make sense of his world. I wouldn't like to have seen me; not the way I looked then. He groaned.

I crossed the room, pulled a grubby yellow sheet from the bed and threw it at Olly Keppard.

"Mop up the ketchup," I said. "It's making me feel sick."

With the slow, lifeless movements of a centenarian scraping burnt toast, Keppard wiped his mouth and tucked some of the sheet into the sling that held his bleeding arm. His face was the color of dried mushrooms. Then he coughed a long time and choked up some of the whiskey.

He called me a bastard again.

I got up, cleaned his mouth with what was left of the water in the can and a corner of the sheet, and put a cigarette between his swollen lips. I put the end of my own to it. Keppard sucked and his Camel lit. I wasn't the S.S. or a power-crazed cop. I was just a private dick with a few questions that, when answered, just might keep me alive. Keppard was enough of a pro to know his game was over. He was a dead man and he knew it. But his death could come later. First he had to bring me glad tidings.

"Why kill Pozo?" I said flatly.

With his free hand Keppard rubbed the sheet over his face and pushed back his hair, which hung like wet bootlaces from his balding dome.

"He knew something." His voice was a gasp.

"And that something had to do with a briefcase belonging to Warren Ratenner," I said.

He nodded. "But I didn't know that at the start of the caper."

He coughed a few short bursts and took the cigarette out of his mouth. Then he spat out some more blood. Pretty soon there was going to be more blood outside Olly Keppard than in him.

"Tell me," I said. "Tell me everything."

"It goes back." He moaned.

"Then go back!" I shouted.

He shifted around and got more or less comfortable. I sat with my arms resting on my legs, leaning forward. It was difficult to hear him.

Keppard said, "I was hanging around Slovan's late one night, a few weeks ago it would be, when this smoothy sidles over and asks me if I could use something thicker than dust to line my pockets with. Seems this bozo got word about me being a real smooth tail. Like me being good enough to stalk a puma. Stalk him with a bell around my neck. Naturally I says I'm interested and I gets a call a day later about some crazy job that involves me swapping a briefcase. It don't sound too promising but the dough seemed worth the clambake."

I nodded. I was all ears.

"The first thing I had to do was take myself down to the Reading Terminal and pick up this special briefcase from the luggage room. When I do this, which is to be a certain time exactly, I got to call a number I been given for my next move. So I twirl the dial a few times and get the ID on two boys who are carrying this special briefcase that I got to swap."

There was a short pause.

"You seen them so you know they ain't no problem to spot."

I nodded some more and dished out some more tobacco. Olly Keppard coughed, winced, blew out smoke and continued.

"I got a swell system. Drive an old yellow cab all hunky-dory with plates and a license which is a gift from some guy

I got something on in City Hall. Means I can get real close without being spotted. No one suspects a tail from an empty cab."

"It puzzled me," I said, "how you did it."

"The info I got," Keppard said, "was that the big goon is heavy on malt and likes to water himself every ten minutes. The plan I got is that when he is funneling the stuff out I do the swap. It ain't a plan I want to patent 'cause the little French guy has sharp little eyes dartin' all over, looking for trouble merchants like myself. Obviously what's in the briefcase is worth more than a barn full of grits."

He had an original way with words, but I didn't interrupt the flow to tell him. I'd drop Ezra Pound a line about it when I got a spare moment. But right now time was shrinking faster than a cheap cotton shirt.

"Tell me about the swap," I said.

"It's coming." He took a deep drag on the cigarette. "I get the break I'm waiting for in a bar behind Rittenhouse Square. The Three Sixes. It's part break, part inspiration. The big goon has sorta filled his tank and heads off to the john. To get the picture you got to understand that the big goon is doing the carrying. The small guy is just the glims and gun."

If it were possible to look pleased with a mouth full of broken teeth, a bullet hole in the arm and a kicked-in stomach, Olly Keppard looked pleased. "Yeah," he said. "The one place a guy gotta have his hands free is in the john."

"So you went into the men's room and found Frank Summers doing his party piece?"

"You wouldn't believe it," he said. "Three goddamn briefcases, each one identical."

"Incredible," I said.

"A real coincidence."

There was a silence then. It was like the moment in the theater between scenes, when the house lights go down and men walk onto the stage and shift the props. But no one came onto our stage. At least no one I heard.

At last I said, "You saw the mix-up and knew the briefcase

Frank Summers had walked off with was the one you wanted. When Summers left, you slid into your taxi, tailed him to Maag's Hotel and while he slept off his jumpy liver you took the case, leaving him a condemned man. Nice work. Then inspiration paid you a second visit. When you found what Frank Summers had found earlier, that the case was worth a sizable share of the Chase Manhattan, you hatched a sweet little scheme all your own. Frank Summers didn't know why he had a lapful of dollar bills and he didn't care. He just wanted them badly enough, needed them badly enough to run. The consequences of doing such a thing never crossed his mind, which was half floating in cocktails and half worn down with financial worry due to his worn-out wife. But you knew the money was hot and you had an inkling where it came from. That there may have been a double-cross somewhere and that the briefcase may have been at the center struck you as a real possibility. You had seen Frenchy playing pool with Joey Pozo. You may have even seen the fixer who gave you the work talking to Frenchy. Either way, when you called in for your next move, the party on the other end of the line had a shock. You weren't asking for orders. You were giving them. Blackmail. The set-up was perfect. There would be no cops and as long as you could convince the guy doing the double-crossing that you knew who owned the case you could ask for the moon."

Keppard's face went grayer than it had ever been, and his eyes widened. He said something I didn't quite hear because of a sudden noise at the side of my head. Like a paper bag full of air being burst. Then I heard voices talking in the distance. Then the voices stopped and there was a muffled crash. And then I was floating away in a gentle, quietly running stream, sinking and rising as the water snaked its way through thick weeds and hard stones. I flapped my arms a few times, and kicked my legs. But I was a drowning man. I looked at the people on the bank and they waved good-bye.

30

He was sprawled across the bed with a pillow over his head. I was sprawled on the carpet with a gun in my hand. My gun. It had been fired very recently. Smoke was still coming out the places smoke comes out of. Most of it was coming out of the barrel. I dragged myself up with my gun still in my hand and staggered like a diver with the bends over to the edge of the bed and flopped. I felt queasy and my head was raw and soggy, like someone had been using it to hammer home tent pegs. The side of my neck was a throbbing, scorching bruise and my trapezius was jumping about like a headless chicken. Someone had sapped me good. I looked over to see what someone had done to Olly Keppard.

In the middle of the pillow was a stain the size of a quarter. A lot of things can leave stains on pillowcases. You can get stains of blueberry jam, axle grease and candle wax. This stain was more of a scorch mark, black near the center and smoking, like someone had carelessly left a cigarette butt there. In the heart of the stain there was a core of red, thick liquid. Liquid like blood. It was steadily welling up and seeping over the scorched and charred cotton, and then sinking into the bag of feathers. Someone had put Olly Keppard's future defense attorney out of work forever.

It was an old trick, using the pillow as a silencer. And an even older one, putting the gun that fired the bullet that killed the man into the hand of the man that owned the gun but didn't do it. But they worked, both tricks, as often as not.

It was as neat a piece of framing as you would ever be likely to see. All the first cop who happened along had to do was pick me up and hang me on the D.A.'s wall. The evidence was everywhere. The bullet in the ceiling, the door half off its hinges, bruises and gore galore, empty bottles of liquor, the bullet in Olly Keppard's temple. It read as easy as a blurb on the flap of a ten-cent novel. And if the D.A. wanted a motive to tidy things up he could always dig out Uglo from Oklahoma City. He would testify that Pozo, killed by Keppard, was my buddy in the war. Revenge would fit the bill perfectly. Open and shut. The jury wouldn't even have time to sit down.

All I needed to finish the frame was the law. And I got them, right on cue.

There were two sirens coming from opposite directions, whining in the sleepy suburban landscape like angry animals along wide, respectable avenues, causing lights to jump on in the faces of cold and silent houses. Dark shapes would appear, pulling back the drawn drapes and starched net curtains. Men in bathrobes with freshly lit cigarettes between their fingers would walk onto their dimly lit porches. They would look inquisitively for a while at the lights flashing across the empty sky, at the vanishing red glow of the tail fins. And set back from the roads, in brick mansions on wooded estates, grumpy men would open one eye and yell at the butler to find out what the hell was going on.

He'd find out that two fast wagons stuffed with fidgety, red-faced cops were coming for Mike Dime, also known as the King of Suckers and the Prince of Dopes. That's what was going on.

The sirens were getting closer. About a mile away. The cops would be fingering their pistols nervously, fussing with things cops fuss with and telling each other to take it easy and not to take chances and to shoot the bastard if he tried any funny business. This wasn't just a local call to break up a rowdy party or step in on someone's domestic beef. This was homicide, a murder one, and the suspect was still on the premises. A crazy killer on the loose with five shots up his sleeve. By the time those cops got to me they'd be about ready to shoot up the whole state.

I put my gun back into its holster and hauled myself off the bed. I crossed the room to the splintered door and edged onto the walkway. Masie Webster was standing by the pool in a housecoat the color of lupines, an ice pack on her head and a drink in her hand. I could hear the siren of the first patrol car, its flashing light twirling furiously above the scraggly shrubs and bushes. Then the blue and white Chevrolet skidded clumsily and much too fast into the driveway. A fender clipped one of the brick pillars and the wheels slid on the oily road. But it kept coming, swaying with the weight of its heavy load, accelerating up what I now saw was quite a sharp incline. That's why I didn't see the pool. That's why the cops didn't see the pool. The tires squealed as the driver tried much too late to change direction. With the clang of buckling metal, the Chevy bounced three times and plunged, like a tin whale, into the pool. Water left the pool like a tidal wave as the big car hit the tiles at the deep end. Filthy water fell by the gallon and drenched everything around, including Masie Webster. Something the size of a frog landed on her neck and jumped off into the night.

The big engine sizzled and fumed under an inch of water while uniformed officers struggled to free themselves from the sinking wagon. The driver was bleeding badly from the face and hands and another man was helping him. One by one they climbed out. They looked unhappy and confused and very wet. As for Masie Webster, she was looking a whole lot better; thinking about four wet cops drying off to Glenn Miller while she fixed them sidecars.

Then the back-up car turned into the drive. It turned in a lot slower. I had no exit at the front of the building so I moved from the doorway and checked out the back. There was a casement window over the toilet big enough to squeeze through. I pushed it open and looked out. There was a row of garbage cans beneath the window, and bits of broken furniture. Some of it would be soft enough to land on, but noisy. The priest's back window was less than three feet away, and open. I closed the lid on the bowl, stepped up, turned around and sat facing the room on the window ledge. I poked an arm out of the window and let my hand creep up the outside wall. My fingertips just made the edge of the parapet that skirted the building a foot below the flat roof. I stretched as far as I could without falling out and bent my fingers into an angled grip. I did the same with my other hand. Carefully I eased myself through the window, bending my legs almost to my chest so I could keep both toes steady on the ledge, braced my arms and straightened up. Then came the tough bit. I stretched out and put my right shoe to the corner of the ledge of the priest's window. Then, my fingers on the brick parapet, I swung across the gap. As soon as both feet were together on the ledge I thrust my arm through the open window and held on by slapping a flat palm against the inside wall. The rest was easy. Getting out in reverse.

I walked to the window and pulled back the curtain. Outside, the boys from the back-up car were busy rigging a searchlight on the roof and a plainclothes dick was messing with a megaphone. The four cops from the first car were standing by the pool. They were wrapped up in blankets and holding drinks.

Suddenly a beam of white light shot upward into the sky like the first flash of a fireworks display, then darted over the wall like a lizard on the run. It held firm, engulfing the door of Keppard's room and part of the priest's front window. The cop with the megaphone was telling men to cover the back of the building and for me to come out with my hands in the air. He said he didn't want any tricks and I was given three minutes to show. If I didn't his men would open fire.

Three minutes. Not a lot of time to do anything much. I could overboil an egg, play Chopin's Minute Waltz a couple of times, run the fastest mile in history. Or I could get out of the frame.

I pulled open the sliding door of Father O'Hanrahan's walk-in closet and rummaged around. There was a topcoat and a cassock and a wide-brimmed hat with a half-ball crown.

There was a dressing table-cum-dresser beneath the front window. It had two large drawers in the belly, two smaller ones at each end of a glass top and a built-in mirror in an oval frame. There was a hairbrush and a comb with some dark hairs between the teeth, an ashtray with three stubs, a missal and a rosary. Not much there for me and the seconds were ticking away as the cop reminded me by yelling out, "Two minutes."

I pulled open a drawer and found a dog collar, some spare socks and some clean underwear.

There was no time to do a complete change of clothing. Not even a vaudeville pro could have done it in two minutes. I took off my jacket and raincoat and pulled the cassock off its hanger and slipped it on. It was three sizes too big around the middle so I rolled up my jacket and raincoat and stuffed them down my front. Then I ringed my neck with the collar, only it immediately flew undone. I pulled a cuff link off my shirt and popped it through the collar stud hole. It didn't look too good, but it didn't look too bad. I stuck the hat on my head and pulled out the bottom drawer of the dresser, which was empty and lined with newspaper.

"One minute and we're coming in," the cop growled.

I took the drawer right out and carried it by the pair of tear-drop handles to the back window. I got a comfortable grip, rammed a corner into the glass pane. Then I threw the drawer down into the trash cans and rattling, crashing hotel junk.

I stepped back into the bedroom just as the first rain of bullets hit the room next door. I belly-dived, rolled into a corner and as loud as my lungs would let me, I shouted,

"'Tis Father O'Hanrahan speaking. For the love of our Savior don't shoot a defenseless priest. A madman has been holdin' me hostage and thrown his poor demented self from the closet window. Have mercy for the sake of your souls."

There was a silence while it all sank in and Masie Webster confirmed that a priest was renting the room. Then the cop with the megaphone told Karnham and Wex to join Bluther and Clinton at the back of the building, and to shoot to kill on sight.

There was the sound of men running beneath the room

and muffled voices as the two cops went off to help search the back.

"Holy Mary, mother of Jesus," I shouted, giving my Barry Fitzgerald all I had. "Put up your guns. I'm coming out."

"Stay where you are, Father," the megaphone said. "There is a homicidal killer at large. You are safer there until we apprehend him."

There was a short pause as one of the cops called from the back of the motel and the detective with the megaphone listened. Then there was a single shot and the yelp of a dog.

I got to my feet and opened the door. The pool of light smacked me in the face, almost blinding me. I put my hand to my eyes. It was the natural thing to do and no one thought anything of it. But the reflex gesture was a bonus to the disguise as my hand and forearm covered almost all my face. I couldn't see the detective as the light was too strong, but he could see me clear as a fish in a glass bowl. And I was well known in Philly law.

"I said stay in your room, Father," the detective called.

I flinched visibly and kept my hand over my face.

"Sure and I heard you," I said. "But there's a boy bein' hunted and 'tis my duty to plead for mercy. We are all sinners in God's eyes, my son, and all of us members of his flock."

I eased down the steps mouthing the platitudes that priests perfect and gradually disengaged myself as the detective's center of interest. Then the spotlight left me and joined the hunting party.

The back-up car was parked facing the pool and the drowned Chevy. A uniformed cop with a rifle was on one knee by the fender of the second car and the detective was casually leaning with both elbows on the roof, holding the megaphone with both hands. He was a big man with big hands and a big enough mouth not to need amplification. The cops who took the plunge were still draped in their blankets and making themselves useful by holding back a handful of local rubbernecks who had appeared from nowhere.

I moved unobtrusively behind the second car and cut along the corner of the pool. My Packard was on the opposite side to the rooms of Keppard and the priest. It was there I bumped into Masie Webster.

"Say, don't I know you?" she said at once, screwing up her eyes and nose. Her bleached hair was hidden under a huge striped cotton towel wrapped like a turban. She still didn't have a brassiere on and it still showed.

"Sure," I said. "I'm Father O'Hanrahan. I live here."

"Nuts," she said and swallowed something from the glass in her hand. "You ain't no priest who lives here and I seen you someplace before." Her voice was sullen and spoiled and just a shade angry. She put a foot toward me and pushed her white, small button of a nose an inch from mine.

"I seen you somewhere, honey," she said. "And it was define-ately not over an altar rail."

Then a look of recognition broke over her puffy and aggressive features. She pulled back her head and opened her jaw. Astonishment fell out. Her larynx was just on the point of shrieking. I watched helpless as the muscles on her thick neck tightened and her throat opened wide enough to play a tuba in. When my right fist clipped her for a second time she spun around on her bare feet three or four times and disappeared over the edge of the pool. There followed a metallic bump, a dismal splash and no scream.

"Lord Jesus have mercy, the lady has thrown herself into the pool," I cried, and backed into the shadow of the porte cochere. There was a lot of shouting and cursing and the still soggy cops started arguing over who should pull La Webster out.

They were still arguing as I crossed the Montgomery County line and was deep enough into Philly to see the red aircraft warning light glowing on the top of City Hall.

31

Thick black smoke rose steadily against a thin, pale sky. In the wreckers' yard, a stone's throw from where Ratenner was waiting for me, three lonely men stood over a pile of smoldering tires. Something crackled in the dying fire and a tongue of flame licked the inside of one of the melting hoops. Sparks jumped out like fluorescent fleas as the fire suddenly revived and the last bits of combustible matter gave themselves up to the flames. The three men stood motionless with their arms outstretched, warming their hands. They were dressed in rags bound with string, like Russian peasants. Two wore tattered hats with dog-chewed brims and holes in the crowns, hats like the ones clowns fool around in. All three had long dirty beards and even dirtier faces, almost featureless with grime. Between them they had less expression than a trio of clay statues. Their eyes focused on a place I could never see, like those on the faces of stuffed animals. It was a place in their past, a place that only few people visit and that, like death, when visited, cannot be related or explained. But it was a place I felt I might be heading toward.

I stepped silently into the circle and opened my palms over the smoke. There was not the faintest breath of wind and the air felt dead. The acrid column of smoke grew high enough to choke the birds.

I wondered what had brought these three ragged men to the edge of the world, what slight change in fortune had led them to the hobo life. Maybe they had been born to it, like great conductors or atomic scientists. A vocation, starting early like Mozart. Instead of composing piano music, at the age of four a hobo would be taking his first boxcar ride. Then at sixteen he'd go bumming on the Bowery and finally graduate with no teeth, lousy skin and consumption. I like hobos. They correct the imbalance of ownership and possession. We need them slightly less than doctors and a whole lot more than movie actors.

One of the two men in hats kicked a charred lump of wood into the embers and spat. The phlegm rolled in the ashes and sizzled. I took out a packet of Camels and handed them around without a word. But when I stuck a hand into the pocket where I kept my lighter I found my billfold instead. It wasn't the pocket I kept my billfold in.

I took it out and examined the contents. Everything was there except the photo I had taken from Frenchy's cadaver. I expected that.

While I was checking out my pockets the man with the muffler picked up a stick and held it in the fire. Then he lifted it and blew the tip. It glowed red and we all leaned forward and took a light. At no time did our eyes meet. Not one man looked directly at another.

I checked my watch. It was eight exactly. The twenty-four hours were up. I didn't have Ratenner's case but I had something better. There were just a few more questions I needed answers to.

"Been here long, boys?" I said.

There was a long pause and then a man said, "Forever."

"Eternity," said another.

"Longer," said the last.

I threw my cigarette into the fire and turned away. They were not the men who had the kind of answers I was looking for.

Ratenner looked pretty much as I had expected him to look. He was sitting behind a table in a high-backed wooden chair under the naked bulb on the top floor of the warehouse where he said he'd be. But he was alone this time. No boys. No guns. Just him and me. He was dressed slightly better than I had imagined from the way he spoke. His suit was good English wool in a muted Prince of Wales check. The lapels were not too wide and, from what I could see, there wasn't too much drape on the jacket. All the stitching was by hand and looked neater than the workings in a Swiss watch. His shirt was silk and so was his tie, a plain maroon without a pin. His pocket handkerchief matched the tie but that looked okay. His hands were well manicured and rested patiently, palms down on the plain wooden table. His cuff links were smaller than most hoods wore but they were still big enough to choke an ostrich. I went and stood close to him. Some of his features were almost familiar. Some less so, like the long, ugly scar that ran the length of his neck on the side they open when a surgeon cuts out a cancer. But his eyes were still the same, hard and evil. Unlike his saggy skin, his wasting muscles and his slowly shrinking body, they were not visibly affected by the change in his blood cells. His hair was sleeked back, as I had seen it, and his mouth had that same twisted look of someone who likes it all his way and snarled whatever way it went. All in all, Warren Ratenner, give or take the swimming pool and the blonde, was the man in Frenchy's photo. It had always puzzled me that a guy like Frenchy should want to carry a picture of his boss and the boss's fluff around with him. It was one of the questions I would have liked Ratenner to answer. But he wouldn't tell me. Not in a million years. The little bullet hole in his left temple said that. There was a scorch mark around the wound, which meant that the gun had been held close, a small-caliber weapon, by the size of the hole. Very tentatively, I laid a single finger on Ratenner's cheek. It was the texture of cheese and quite cold. Blood had congealed around the wound and formed a black scab. He had been dead for hours.

There were things I had to do.

I unbuttoned his jacket, felt for his wallet, looked carefully at its contents and learned no more than I knew already. I went through his other pockets and found a pair of brand-new Yale keys on a gold ring threaded through a big black onyx die with ivory spots. The keys were identical, made to fit the main door to a house or apartment. They had been hardly used. You could tell that by the small slivers of fresh-cut metal still clinging to the jagged grooves. There was nothing else at all in Warren Ratenner's pockets. I kept ahold of the keys and took a look around the room.

It was long and high and had more lights than were being used. But there was enough light to see. At the end of the room, along the far wall, stood a line of industrial cupboards, which were unlocked with their doors wide open. There were a few three-drawer filing cabinets and a hand-operated printing press on a metal table. The press was well maintained and had been used often and recently. There were some blank strips of trimmed paper and cardboard on the floor and a lot more piled in a metal bin. There was nothing in the cupboards but unopened packages of printing paper of various sizes and quality, and used bottles of ink. You couldn't have got more than a hundred and fifty bucks for the whole works.

I fished around the junk in the bottom drawer of one of the filing cabinets and found a leather-bound ledger. The completed pages had been torn out and only half a single column of the one page that remained was filled in. The figures added up to the usual mishmash that only accountants make sense of. All I could tell was that the figures were large. They could have been dollars, or they could have been jars of Doctor Jolly's Wart Cream.

Either way, it didn't matter much.

I threw the mutilated book back into the drawer, turned off the light and said adios to the late Warren Ratenner.

If I put my foot down, I would just catch Elaine Damone before she left town.

32

She was standing with her back to me in her soft, all-pink bedroom, taking clothes from a rosewood cupboard and packing them swiftly and neatly into two red pigskin suitcases. She was surprised to see me. Her big black almond eyes flashed and blinked. And then she stopped what she was doing. Stopped dead.

"Traveling light?" I said, walking into the room.

"Mike Dime," Elaine Damone said in total disbelief. "What are you doing here? How on earth did you get in?"

I threw Ratenner's keys onto the unmade bed. She followed their trajectory through the air and stared hard as they landed with a faint clink in the folds of the pink silk sheets.

She was holding the bundle of chicken wire and half a yard of spotted satin that *Vogue* was calling a "millinery creation" that year. She took a tissue-lined hatbox from a shelf in the cupboard and carefully put the hat in it.

She was looking unbearably lovely in a white, full-length cotton nightgown with slightly raised shoulders and full sleeves gathered generously at the wrists. With its high-cut bodice it would have been considered a chaste, somewhat virginal garment. But a large scarlet dragon in Chinese silk emblazoned high over the right breast put an end to that.

There was a dust sheet over the only easy chair. It was facing the door of the bedroom. I crossed the room and, without removing the sheet, sat down.

"How long have you known?" Elaine Damone said, emptying a drawer.

She turned to me again, some silk underwear in her hand. It was the very latest thing from the very latest place rich women go to buy things. From the line of her nightgown I could see she didn't have any on her body. There was something in Elaine Damone's other hand that interested me almost as much as the lingerie. It was a pretty little Walther PP, a .32 with a nicely engraved barrel, oak leaves and acorns, and a pearl grip. There was a black mark at the nozzle where I guessed it had been recently fired, probably into Warren Ratenner's head.

"Keep your hands out of your pockets," she said with a voice cold enough to take the heat out of a chili. "And leave them where I can see them."

I did what she said.

"Grant a condemned man a last cigarette?" I said. She lifted the small gun, held it with both hands and pointed it at a spot between my eyes.

"There are seven cartridges in a fully loaded gun of this make. There are still five left, and I wouldn't need more than one to kill you. Smoke by all means, if that is how you wish to spend your last minutes alive. But first there are one or two things I want to know. I thought I had created a completely foolproof plan, but apparently there were loopholes. In order that they do not occur again, I would like to know what you have discovered."

I took out a cigarette very slowly, lit it and sucked hard. The smoke hit my toes but it didn't make me feel any better. Elaine Damone might have been put together like a woman. All the fleshy bits were there and all of them in just the right places. But her heart or her soul or whatever the damn thing is called was stone. My one hope of staying alive depended on how long I could keep my tongue wagging. I was going to tell her the whole story and I was going to make her enjoy listening to it. But there was something special I was going to keep till the end, a sort of postscript. I wasn't sure it would fit. But it was my only chance.

I said, "It might take a while."

"Don't waste more breath than you have to. I don't have all day."

Elaine Damone moved out from behind the bed, pushed the seat from under the dressing table with a bare foot and sat facing me with her back to the door. Her hair was still uncombed. It fell in graceful, heavy waves, masking half her face and covering most of one dark eye.

Elaine Damone let the hand holding the gun slip down into her lap. She parted her long legs wide beneath her nightgown and pressed the bottom of the grip firmly between them, just below the Venus mound. My mouth went dry and I twitched so violently I almost dropped my Camel.

"It was the picture frame," I said. "The one you used to have on the mantelpiece in the living room."

I was made almost speechless by the position of Elaine Damone's gun hand. But I went on with my story.

"It was your only mistake," I said. "But it had more to do with your personality than your plan. You are one woman in a million. The way you dress, the stuff you fill your place with, even the way you make love."

"Tell me something I don't know," she said with a contented smile.

"Everything about you is perfect," I said. "There's not one single blemish on the whole of your fabulous body. That kind of perfection is both beautiful and sick. Not only in the attainment but also in the finished product. There was no sense in your having put a picture frame on the mantelpiece and not having a picture in it. I didn't know at that time why it was empty. Nor did you know for sure when you picked me up after Warren's boys piled up the Buick that I was the private eye Warren wanted to talk to. But when you shook me down before sending my grubby old suit to the cleaners, you found a picture I had taken from a dead Frenchman. A picture of your boss and a blonde."

I had finished the cigarette and looked around for an ashtray. There wasn't one at hand so I squeezed out the burning end between my thumb and forefinger and put the butt tidily on the arm of the chair.

When I looked at Elaine Damone there was something different. The gun was in the same place, nestling in the dark crevasse at the top of her thighs, but her cotton nightgown was up around the top of her thighs. No nakedness was ever more beautiful. Her breathing was fast and clearly audible from where I sat.

"Go on," she said. "You sound almost interesting."

I did what I could to resume the diary of Elaine Damone.

"You probably won't remember our bathing together," I said. "I'm not much of a match compared with the stock of a German .32. But afterward, while you were busy in here with Coco Chanel and Helena Rubinstein, I was busy with Papa Hemingway in the living room. For a reason I still don't understand I went over to your bookcase and pulled the guy off the shelf. I say I don't understand because Ernie does nothing for me. I prefer the pulp boys for big talk. They're funnier and they don't philosophize about being tough. Thinking back, I seem to remember that the spine of the book was a fraction out of line with the others. Perhaps that was it. Anyway, I sat down and opened it up. There was nothing unusual about the book. It had all the standard things you find in a full-leather, hand-bound volume. It was beautifully tooled, had boards, endpapers, silk headbands and lots of pages with words on them. There was also a picture, but it wasn't one the publishers had included. It was a picture like one I had seen before, of a man sitting by a pool in a sunny spot like they have on the West Coast. He was a hard-eyed bastard with a nasty grin and a tumor in his throat. There was a woman next to him. In the photo I got from Frenchy she was blonde and not much more. But she had a replacement in your photograph, and an inscription scrawled over her legs: 'To my tootsie, Elaine.'"

The woman with the gun made a noise in the back of her throat, like she was spitting. She said, "I would vomit every time he touched me."

"That's tough," I said. "I only had his boys touch me, and they just thumped me senseless."

Elaine Damone laughed. A heartless empty laugh for me. But something ecstatic for her.

"Imagine," she said. "You knowing all along."

"Knowing is one thing," I said. "But proving is another. Besides, at that time I was still the hunted."

"And you decided to play it that way?" she said. "Hoping you could lead the hunter to your lair?"

I nodded and she pressed the handle of the gun deeper into her body. She seemed to shiver slightly.

"You fell for the Stanton Damone story," she said, her eyes almost closed.

"We'll talk about Stanton Damone later," I said. "First tell me why Frenchy carried a picture of his boss around in his billfold?"

"You are a simpleton," she said. "Charming in your own rough way. But a fool for all that. The blonde was Frenchy's sister, the little tramp. Warren thought he was in love with her until I came into his life."

"So you joined up with Ratenner and his front man Eddie Holland. Ratenner spent a lot of dough keeping you happy, and having Eddie Holland around when the boss was out of town wasn't so bad either. But you had other plans than just sitting around swimming pools. And you found out that Teddy had some of the same. As the front man, Holland handled the money. That made it halfway a cinch. When Ratenner closed down an operation the capital doubled. When he was through with Philly, it was a fortune. It was time to make your move. You sold Holland the idea you were nuts over him and persuaded him to double-cross his boss. You got him to string in a small-time hotel sneak called Olly Keppard. His job was to swap the briefcase after the liquidation of funds following the murder of the insurance man, Kirkpatrick. But it went wrong. First Keppard lost his chance to swap the briefcase without anyone knowing. And later, when he found out what was going on, you found yourself at the end of a blackmail bid. Then it went right again. You found me."

I was getting to the end and no one had shown. Not the U.S. cavalry, not my fairy godmother, and I couldn't see an Avon rep with a loaded bazooka anywhere. Scheherazade had kept her hubby from feeding her to the ants by telling him a story and holding back the punch line. She kept the same story going a thousand and one nights. I hoped I had half her luck.

"Olly Keppard got greedy. He didn't want just a slice

of the cake, he wanted the oven, the mill, the whole damn bakery. You fed me a line about your brother being blackmailed. But it was you."

Elaine Damone threw back her head and laughed. She took the gun from between her legs and bit the back of the hand holding it. Her legs were open as wide as legs can ever be and I tried not to stare. Then she stood up suddenly and the hem of the thin cotton gown fell back to the floor, leaving sharp creases in the places where the gown had been folded. Saliva trickled from the corner of her mouth and her breathing was fitful, her eyes blazing with a terrible narcissism. That's what it looked like to me and that's what it had to be in order for me to eke out a few more minutes. Help was on the way In the dark passage leading to the bedroom, something stirred.

"Your brother was a fake," I said. "Just as you are. There is no Damone family. I checked it out. No Damones in Brazil. No Damones in Argentina or Peru or El Salvador or anywhere else in South America."

"But I am very real," she breathed. "And you can see, very much alive. And now I am going away."

"But you haven't heard the rest of the story. There is no fun in being so clever if you don't know that someone else knows just how. You can kill me anytime, but once I am dead you will never know how much I knew."

She was holding the gun steady, but she was listening hard.

I went on quickly.

"You sent Holland to pay me off. You figured I'd drawn a blank and wasn't going to get you your briefcase. I was in the way. Holland struck lucky. He arrived just as I was cracking Joey Pozo's code and he had the sense to take it all in. Then he tailed me to the Abington Motel, sapped me and stuck me in a frame. That was when it became clear he was your boy and not Ratenner's. Then, I assume, he brought the briefcase back here while you were out killing Ratenner. Then you shot Teddy Holland."

"All men are disposable." Elaine Damone laughed again and lifted the gun at arm's length. "By the way," she said, "Holland killed Ratenner. I didn't. I was here all night, sleeping like a newborn child. But that aside, your summing up has been worth the wait. In another life you might have been worth something to me. Such a skillful deduction of events should not be rewarded with nothing more than a sudden death. But that, my dear Mr. Dime, is your fate."

She released the safety catch and started to squeeze the trigger.

33

Two metal rims, each an inch and a half across, crawled along the faded rose carpet and grew into tubes each about a foot long. They in turn became a wooden stock that was attached to the shoulder of a bleeding, dying man. He was dressed the same way as I had seen him the night before, when he came into my office and warned me off. Except that then he didn't have a bullet hole above his heart. If Elaine Damone had not been so busy telling me about fate she would have heard Teddy Holland struggling along the floor on his stomach. But all she heard was the echo of the blast from a single barrel of Holland's sawed-off shotgun. The force of the blast was so great it blew Elaine Damone clear across the room and directly into my arms. We staggered, she sagged and we didn't quite fall. And Elaine Damone made no sound, not one. She died staring helplessly at me with her big almond eyes wide open.

I looked over her shoulder, flinching, expecting a second blast. But Holland was finished with shooting people. He lay at full stretch with the shotgun smoking quietly beside him.

I danced Elaine Damone's body to the bed and laid her on it. The scarlet dragon on the breast of her nightgown was changing shape, spreading as the dead woman's blood penetrated the purest of white cottons. There was a lot of blood. It poured from her nose and it poured from her mouth. Blood seemed to be pouring from everywhere.

I felt the room go cold and my heart was pounding louder than a bass drum in a New Orleans parade. I think there must have been a mist in the room because I couldn't see clearly.

I stood watching the dragon until it had no more shape and there was not one moving, living thing left in the whole of Elaine Damone's beautiful body. Then I bent over her and pulled down the lids of her eyes and I think I may have kissed her because there was warm sticky blood on my mouth when I straightened up.

Holland hadn't arrived a moment too soon. Of course, he had been there all the time, dying in Elaine Damone's living room. She had shot Holland above the heart and then left him to bleed to death. But he wasn't quite dead when I passed by. His gun was on the piano. All he had to do was to get the gun, crawl along the carpet to the bedroom, and . . .

I was sick of it. I sat down on the bed beside Elaine Damone's corpse, wiped my hands on a sheet and picked up the phone from the night table. I dialed downtown and waited. It was Sunday morning, a little after ten o'clock. People were going to church, weeding their gardens, glancing through newspapers. The whole of Philadelphia was doing something, but nobody was answering the phone in the Germantown police precinct.

With my idle hand I absently dipped into one of the suitcases Elaine Damone had been busy packing. Under some dresses I found the briefcase. It was strange seeing it at last. I got the same sensation as bumping into an old flame at a party, or meeting a school pal in a distant country. But I didn't touch it; I was more interested in an old family photo album covered in a yellowing, floral wallpaper packed carefully beside it. I picked up the book, rested it on my knees and let the pages fall open one by one. Each picture was identical in size, the unassuming square of an old box camera. The faces in all the pictures were of one family. Dark hair and almond eyes were everywhere. The last picture in the book was bigger than the others and had a professional's touch. It also had a caption. The photograph showed a large family group of sharecroppers dressed in black. Behind the line of children standing tallest to smallest was an endless horizon of dirt. There was more dirt in the foreground. One grown man headed the parade, dressed in a stiff-looking suit and starched collar. His face was less like his girls, more like the boys, but drawn with worry. It looked beaten and drained by the interminable, desperate struggle to make something of the dirt around him. There was also a dilapidated barn and a rickety, clapboard shack with smoke coming from a brick chimney. There was not a lot else except the sadness on the faces of the family. And there wasn't a mother. The nicely written but childish hand said so. It said, "The day ma died and was buried."

There were eleven kids on parade. The middle one, a girl, lay dead beside me.

No one answered me downtown. But by then I didn't want to talk to anyone, except maybe an understanding woman or a priest who hadn't heard of sin. I didn't know either one.

I put the receiver carefully in its cradle and placed the photo album on Elaine Damone's breast, so it covered the stain. Then I got up and walked slowly through the empty apartment with all its crazy dreams and opened the door.

The noise I made slamming it woke the whole goddamn world.